DELIVER US FROM EVIL

DELIVER US FROM EVIL

✦

A World War II Novel

DANIEL REED

iUniverse, Inc.

New York Lincoln Shanghai

Deliver Us From Evil
A World War II Novel

Copyright © 2006 by Daniel Reed

iUniverse, Inc.

iUniverse books may be ordered through booksellers or by contacting:

iUniverse
2021 Pine Lake Road, Suite 100
Lincoln, NE 68512
www.iuniverse.com
1-800-Authors (1-800-288-4677)

This is a work of fiction. All of the characters, names, incidents, organizations and dialogue in this novel are either the products of the author's imagination or are used fictitiously.

ISBN-13: 978-0-595-39678-8 (pbk)
ISBN-13: 978-0-595-84084-7 (ebk)
ISBN-10: 0-595-39678-X (pbk)
ISBN-10: 0-595-84084-1 (ebk)

Printed in the United States of America

PROLOGUE

Over four hundred thousand German and Italian prisoners of war were stationed throughout the United States during the Second World War. They began arriving in November of 1942 to be safely confined and to work in jobs vacated by American servicemen who were away fighting overseas. There were 126 prisoner of war (i.e., POW) camps in America, each housing several thousand men.

This story takes place in May of 1943. Two lone guards lead thirteen German POWs from Camp Trinidad in the extreme south of Colorado to the Segundo Coal Mines snuggled into the magnificent Rocky Mountains an hour up the road. To say that security is lax is an understatement, but this is the norm in all POW camps throughout the United States. After all, where are these men to go if they do escape? Few know English, and none possesses the stamina to swim the Atlantic.

From Monday to Friday each week, the POWs make the two-hour trek to the mines, work their six-hour shift, and then march back to the prison camp. The POWs, mostly seasoned soldiers of Rommel's legendary Africa Korps, are clothed in distinctive khaki fatigues with a bright yellow "PW" emblazoned on their backs.

1

The early morning air was damp and cold under an overcast sky, the eastern hori-zon a broad unbroken plain, a veritable grandeur. Fir trees with fresh green tips hugged the mountain roads, and vibrant wallflowers and mariposa lilies were resplendent in the valleys where the thin gray morning mist lay.

A light rain had begun as burly, bull-necked U.S. Army Corporal Vince Boe and weedy, teenaged Private Aaron Radmanovich escorted their German POW work crew along Highway 22.

The German's senior officer, Colonel Helmut Von Toth, was a fine specimen cut from Prussian aristocracy. In his late forties, he was tall and striking, rock hard, and heavy jawed with short-cut grayish black hair. A cold, silent man with deep-set restless eyes, he marched up the highway at a proud military gait with the others in the detail. A peacetime professor of English at the University of Dresden, he knew the American language like his own.

"We'd be honored to favor you men with a request," said Von Toth. The POWs had just finished a grand rendition of their national anthem and were eager for more.

"I ain't heard 'Lili Marlene' yet today, Colonel," replied Boe in his yawning Georgian drawl.

The Germans grabbed up the tune and happily obliged, belting out their favorite song to the delight of their lighthearted guards.

At its completion, Colonel Von Toth called ahead, "Corporal Boe, may I have a word with you?"

Boe obliged, leaving Radmanovich to lead the column as he fell back with Von Toth. Conversing with the German officer had become one of his favorite pastimes these last months—just behind getting the better of him at chess in Camp Trinidad's recreation hall. "What's on your mind?" he said.

"Nothing more than what you Americans refer to as a 'bull session.' I can't expect to master this language of yours without practice."

"They tell me back at camp you've taken over teachin' the English class, Colo-nel. Maybe I ought to be takin' lessons from you."

3

"Your language has always fascinated me. Indeed, one finds it most difficult to travel abroad without it these days. It's absolutely wonderful of your government to offer my men English lessons. We have a lot of time on our hands here, and we might as well be learning something of use for when this war's finally run its course. How about you? Any interest in foreign languages?"

"Me? I know but one foreign word, and I cain't use it in polite company."

"Really, Vince, you must do something about that slang. *Cain't* isn't a word. Nor is *ain't*."

"Yeah, and you remind me too much of my grade school teachers back home, Colonel. Get off my case, would you?"

Von Toth playfully slapped his keeper's shoulder and chuckled. "I'm only—as you Yanks say—*pulling your leg*. You know that."

"So you're really serious about stayin' on in America when this war's over?" asked Boe.

"Dead serious. I fell in love with your country when I visited New York with my parents in 1911. It was then that I started learning English. The bloody Nazis have destroyed my Germany. I no longer want any part of it."

"Well, I wish you the best. You'd make a fine American citizen, Colonel."

Von Toth struck a match, sheltered it behind his cupped left hand, lit two cigarettes, and handed one to Boe. He removed his cap and lifted his face to the light rain, inhaling deeply and speaking with smoke trailing out his nose and mouth. "Corporal, I would like to present you with something that was once very dear to me." He removed the Iron Cross dangling from his neck and handed it to Boe. "Please accept it as a token of my respect and friendship over these last months. You've made my stay at Trinidad a pleasant one."

Boe received the coveted medallion with awe. "Your Iron Cross? Why, I cain't accept this. This is a medal of *honor*. You earned it on the battlefield with Rommel at Tobruk."

"No, please take it. It means nothing to me now. It was won in the service of a country I no longer respect. Please—it would mean a lot to me if you would accept it."

"I don't know what to say, Colonel."

"How about 'thank you'? If nothing else, you could always pawn it after the war."

"Why, sure I'll have it, but I ain't gonna *pawn* it. I'll keep it always … you know…to remind me of our friendship here. And say, Colonel, I been meanin' to tell you. There's lots of good places to live in these United States. But I tell you,

Georgia's the best by far. I'd be pleasured to have you livin' next to me in Tocoa Falls someday. Prettiest doggone place in the whole world."

Von Toth extended his hand to shake Boe's and answered in an imitation Southern drawl to match his companion's. "Well, that would make Georgia my first choice then."

A smile engulfed Boe's big fleshy face. "Well all righty, then. Done deal. And thanks ... thanks a million for this here medallion!"

"The pleasure is mine, my friend."

The POWs had moved on into a German folk song totally unfamiliar to their guards, though Private Radmanovich was swinging his bayonet like a baton in time with the singing.

"Aaron, this is as good a place as any for a rest," beckoned Corporal Boe.

"You got my vote on that," replied Radmanovich as he called a halt.

Suddenly the rain and the cloud cover were gone. The sun came out, and all around, color returned; the green of the pine and fir, the blue of the spruce and columbine, and the red of the graveled road.

The men sank to the rain-moistened earth; almost all lit cigarettes and lay back to enjoy the jagged white mountain peaks now visible to the west and sun-bathed forest to the south.

Von Toth's big, beefy German sergeant, Julius Straub, found a place near Boe and Von Toth. As he sat, he kept his eyes on the two, as if waiting for something.

Radmanovich sat next to his favorite of the bunch, Georg Dreschler, a handsome young man with warm, Nordic blue eyes and an innocent smile. "Cigarette?" Radmanovich asked him, extending his pack.

"No, no thank you," replied Georg in a quiet baritone. "I haven't much taste for them."

Georg was a thin young man, who, in spite of his light blue eyes, had a swarthy complexion and coal black hair. He spoke flawless English, his London-born mother having moved to Germany in her late teens. In fact, it was his knowledge of the English language that had landed him in Hitler's army, which had made Georg, at the tender age of sixteen, an interpreter for frontline enemy prisoners of war.

To say Georg was out of place in German uniform was an understatement. He was gentle, sensitive, and compassionate—qualities not held in high regard in the military, especially in the belligerent, desperate German military of 1943. Yet these words described this young man to a T. He made it no secret that he aspired to a teaching certificate back home when this awful war had run its course.

Radmanovich lay back on the damp earth, crossed his hands behind his head, and looked at Georg, wondering. "You been skittish as a March hare all mornin'," he said. "Somethin' eatin' you?"

Georg was taken back by the question. He stared anxiously at the untroubled leaves of a young aspen overhead. He fumbled his reply. Yes, something was "eating him," but he couldn't tell Radmanovich what it was. "Why no ... no, nothing. Just a bit ... homesick is all. I'll be fine. Don't worry."

Radmanovich chuckled. "Shucks, I ain't worried. No skin off my nose." He shook his head and looked at his German buddy. "I just can't get over it. The German Army appears at your door on a Friday; ships you off to North Africa with no military training whatsoever on Saturday; you arrive in the desert on Monday; your division surrenders on Tuesday; and you're on a POW ship bound for the United States on Thursday."

"That's correct." Georg smiled at his friend.

"One heckuva military career, is all I got to say."

Georg stared at the aspen leaf he was spinning by its stem between his thumb and forefinger. "I was being fitted for this uniform when the news arrived that our commander had just surrendered to your army. I can't say I was terribly disappointed. I knew our situation there in Tunis was hopeless, and I'd seen enough of our dead and wounded those three days to hope for a way out of the war altogether."

Radmanovich laughed. "You've got a great war story there to tell the kids someday, huh? 'There I was buttonin' up my britches when the call came to lay down our arms and surrender.' You're a bloody war hero, Georg!"

Georg kept his gaze on the leaf. All he could think of was his beautiful home, his loving parents. And in his mind, he asked, *And after today, what will become of me?*

Corporal Boe, who had been eavesdropping, remarked, "Just think, Georg. If you hadn't caught a hair in your pants zipper that day, you would've escaped this confounded war without a scratch."

"Are you Americans always so rude to your guests?" asked the smiling Georg, a little embarrassed at Boe's vulgarities.

"Most of the time," answered Boe. "So tell me, Georg, are you plannin' like your colonel here on stayin' on in this great country of ours when this war's over?"

Georg looked up quickly at Boe, wishing he could tell him what he knew. "I was not aware of my colonel's plans to stay here after the war."

"Yup. Him and me are gonna start us the finest diner in all of Tacoa Falls. Huh, Colonel?"

Von Toth smiled. "Whatever you say, *partner*. How about it Georg? Why not stay on with me here once the war is over?"

"Thank you, but no, sir. I plan to return to my family in Stuttgart."

2

"All right, boys. Up and at 'um," bellowed the big-stomached Boe as he took to his feet. "I know you fellas just cain't wait to breathe in that wonderful coal dust up at the mine. Come on, Weber, Dreibech. Straub, that means you too."

As Straub rose from the ground, Boe did not notice the evil glare in the big man's eyes.

With the overcast gone, the high country Colorado sun burned bright and hot. Aside from those clouds lingering around the mountain peaks, only wisps remained. The landscape was hushed and soft under a wondrous blue sky, a God-blessed profound mountain peace. Songbirds perched in spruce branches overhanging the road and heralded the delicious spring morning.

Von Toth joined Boe as they trudged on along the road to the mines, the red gravel crunching beneath the hard waffled soles of their boots.

"I still cain't figure an officer up and volunteerin' for this grunt work when you could be back at camp lyin' around in the sun like a true gentleman," said Boe.

"Just look at this scenery," answered the colonel. He spread his arms in a melodramatic gesture, threw back his head, and shutting his eyes and mouth, sucked in a deep breath through his nose. He opened his eyes again and pointed. "See them? See them, Vince? The Sangre De Cristos—'The Blood of Christ?' You'd have me sitting behind barbed wire back at Trinidad and *missing* all this?"

The big man chuckled. "The way I look at it, you got six hours of shovelin' filthy black coal in a cold, miserable mine shaft to look forward to. Is *that* worth this scenery?"

"I am a man of *action*, Corporal. You may as well put a bullet in my brain as to ask me to sit around that camp all day."

"Well, like the farmer who kissed his cow said, 'to each his own.' God bless you for your work ethic, Colonel." The mountain road had grown steep and he was panting now.

"So tell me, Vince. There's talk back at camp of a magnificent cattle ranch in these parts. Do you know of it?"

"Oh, yeah. I know it, all right. The Carson place. It's run by Jack Carson, an honest-to-goodness mountain man if I ever seen one."

"A '*mountain* man'?"

"Yeah. A throwback to the old west, that one. Dresses and acts like he just stepped off some Hollywood movie set."

"You've met this man?"

"Met him? Why, he's a friend of mine. I know him well. Well…only for these past eight months since they sent me out here, but I play cards with the man once a week. And I was out huntin' with him last November. He's an outfitter and trail guide, the best in all Colorado, they say—a descendent of the great *Kit* Carson. You know, the famous hunter and army scout, Kit Carson. You heard of him, ain't you?"

"Can't say that I have. I'm not much up on my American history, I'm afraid. It sounds like this Carson fellow is quite a man."

"Yup. Ranchin', fishin', guidin', huntin'. You name it, he does it."

"Well, I should think he must have a considerable number of horses to tend to on such a fine spread."

"Yes, sirree. Better than forty head of the finest mounts in the West."

"I hear it's a beautiful ranch."

"It's truly a sight to behold, Colonel. He built him a new ranch house just before his wife passed a few years back. It's the most gorgeous place in these parts. Set back in the woods at the base of a snowcapped mountain. Pretty as a picture. People come out this way just to get a look at it."

"I'd give anything to see it … maybe after the war."

Boe slapped his companion on the back. "Hey, this here country ain't got nothin' on the Appalachians back in Georgia. If nothin' else, you just gotta come visit me there sometime."

Von Toth lit another smoke and became silent, adrift in his thoughts of how this buffoon and his speech and his slaps on the back and his presumption of friendship irritated him. He looked despondently at the dull red of the graveled road before him: what an image of desolation!

Boe gave him a long, hard look. "What's wrong, Colonel? I say somethin' to upset you?"

"No, nothing, my friend. It's just that I miss my freedom so. You undoubtedly take yours for granted, but these last months I've realized just how precious my liberty to come and go really was."

Boe felt sorry for the man. "Cheer up, Colonel. Like you said earlier, you got all this scenery to enjoy. Fresh air, exercise—what more could you want?"

"Vince, I...I don't suppose you'd consider allowing us a glimpse of that Carson place?" As he spoke, Von Toth caught Straub looking at him with a flash of excitement in eyes.

Boe said, "Why, you're really taken up with that ranch, ain't you?"

"I've always dreamed of owning a place like Carson's, and I'd dearly love just a quick look, that's all."

"Colonel, you gotta understand; my arse would be in a sling if I took you fellas on a detour without permission from my captain. Tell you what; I'll talk to him when we get back tonight. Maybe he'll let us go to the Carson's later this week."

Afraid he couldn't hide his irritation another minute, Von Toth sighed and looked away. "Corporal, you know what the policy is on these matters—no sightseeing for POWs, no special arrangements."

"Aw, shucks. Rules was made to be broke. My captain's a fair-minded man. He may be willing to look the other way on something like this."

Shucks? Von Toth thought. *How much more of this idiot can I take?* He forced a friendly but disappointed air. "No. No, he won't, Vince. But there I go again, head in the clouds. Sometimes I forget that I'm a prisoner of war with *no* rights, much less privileges. I'm sorry I brought it up." With this, Von Toth patted Boe on the shoulder and dropped back to walk with his men, exasperated with this fool, but feigning disappointment.

Boe hated to see his good friend drop back. The colonel seemed to be in a funk today, impatient and a little on the foul side. Boe fingered the Iron Cross dangling from his neck, and shame came over him. Couldn't he put the rulebook away just this once? Yeah. Sure he could!

He stepped out of line, stopped, placed his hands on his hips, and called ahead to his subordinate. "Aaron, take your next left. We're gonna treat these boys to a look-see of the Carson Ranch."

Von Toth felt the thrill of success and grinned at Boe.

"The Carson Ranch?" countered Radmanovich, his freckled face wrinkled in a knot. "What in tarnation do you wanna go do a fool thing like that for? If the captain catches us up there, he'll have our butts for breakfast."

"You argue any more with me and I'll have yours for lunch today, Private. Now I'll take full responsibility. Just do as I tell you and go left at the next road. You hear me?"

"I hear you. But the captain'll be likely to take away our liberty for the entire month of June if he finds out."

Boe fell in line next to Von Toth, holding out the extended fingers of his left hand, his voice firm. "Five minutes, Colonel. That's all you get. Five minutes, and then we're off like a new bride's nightie. Understand?"

"I understand, Vince, and thank you; thank you very much," replied Von Toth. He extended his right hand and vigorously shook Boe's.

"Well, this wouldn't be the first time I wound up in the captain's office if we do get caught, and it certainly won't be the last."

"I don't suppose we'll have the good fortune of seeing Jack Carson himself out roping cattle or mending fence?"

Boe chuckled. "I wouldn't get my hopes up if I was you. He's more likely to be out hunting bear with some city slickers this time of year."

"This Jack Carson appears to be one tough individual."

Again Boe laughed, lightly shaking his head. "Yeah, he's tough all right, but folks say they've only ever seen him mad once—about a year ago now. His oldest boy, Wade, got into a ruckus with a boy at school. They was each about seventeen. Got the better of him, Wade did. Well, this here other boy's daddy—a hard-livin' logger from up Starkville way—he decided to make things right with Wade. Both boys had been suspended from school, and word got out that the other boy's daddy was gonna take care of young Wade the day they was let back in. Well, Jack Carson ain't one to never start no fight, but he ain't the kind of man who's gonna sit back and watch one of his boys get whupped by a full-grown man neither. So he showed up after school that day, and half the cotton-picking town turned out to watch the fight. Neither man was gonna back away, so they went at it right there on the school grounds. Old Jack and that logger near killed one another, but when it was done, Jack was the last one standin'. He up and helped that logger to his feet and shook his hand like there was no hard feelings."

"Sounds like you don't mess with Jack's children," said Von Toth.

Boe replied, "You'd do better messin' with a mama bear's cubs."

3

The bluff overlooking the Carson Ranch offered the finest view of the impressive dwelling. The magnificent ranch house stood in a grove of majestic blue spruce at the foot of a splendid snowcapped mountain. The outbuildings and corrals, immaculately kept, lay on the edge of a fertile plain watered by little creeks that came down from the surrounding mountains. The sightseers stood atop the bluff whipped by a chilly breeze strong enough to put a charge into the cedar limbs about them.

Gazing down, Colonel Von Toth put on his best imitation of Southern twang. "Corporal Boe, I can see ya'll weren't just whistlin' Dixie when you said just how beautiful this place was."

Georg was standing beside Boe, trying to keep his revulsion at Von Toth's stupid display from showing on his face. But he said, "Yes. This is truly a sight to behold."

"Especially pretty this time of year, with the leaves just coming out and all," Boe replied.

"What I wouldn't give for a camera right now," gushed Von Toth, within himself smiling smugly at his success. "So incredibly lush and green!"

"You sayin' your country ain't got nice sights like this?" inquired Radmanovich, reaching for a smoke in his shirt pocket.

"Oh, yes, I assure you it does, Private. But it seems so very long now since I've had the opportunity to appreciate such beauty. This pathetic conflict has stolen my very soul."

"Well, drink it in, Colonel," said Boe, helping himself to one of Radmanovich's cigarettes. "You're on the clock now, and you ain't likely to get another peek anytime soon."

Von Toth sat down on a boulder and gulped the fresh mountain air as though he'd never before tasted anything like it. "Oh, that the war would end tomorrow, and we could get back to living like civilized human beings again," he said.

At this, Georg turned away in disgust.

Boe ambled over and placed his boot atop the same boulder.

From a few yards away, Georg regarded Boe's granite features and bulldog body outlined against the rugged backdrop—regarded them with something like pity.

Boe drew heavily on his cigarette and said, "I'm afraid your boys back in Europe got a bit more fight left in 'um yet. You'd best not get too fired up about any world peace for a spell. I hear Hitler's got the friggin Russkies stopped in their tracks, and there ain't no sign of the Allies invadin' France anytime soon."

Von Toth nodded. "Yes, this war is far from over, but at least it's over for me and my men. I suspect my government will soon sign an armistice forcing us to give back everything we've won these past years. What a horrible waste of precious humanity!"

"Armistice?" Boe said. "That's not the way I hear it! The Allies say they'll accept nothing less than unconditional surrender. No terms, nothing to haggle over. Just drop your dang guns and go home."

"That seems a touch arrogant of your side, wouldn't you say, Corporal? I mean, Germany still holds the upper hand in Russia, and your armies aren't exactly having an easy time of it in Italy. I should think the Allies would welcome an end to the fighting with dignity for all."

"Well, looky here, Colonel." Boe gestured with his big hands. "You've changed colors since we last talked. What was all this about America bein' in the right and Nazi Germany bein' the bad guys and all?"

"Oh, I assure you, Corporal, I haven't changed my feelings in the least. I still believe in your country's just cause. I'm only saying your people could save a great deal of bloodshed and suffering by offering to sit down with my government and work out a just peace. After all, I'm sure you wouldn't want all of Europe overrun by the despicable Communists, would you?"

"I reckon not, but I think it's best to deal with one devil at a time. We'll put the Commies in their place when the time comes." Boe threw down his cigarette and ground it beneath his boot. Then, he straightened his back and stretched his arms skyward, yawning deeply. "Well, time's about up, boys. Take one last look, and we'll make for the mines double quick."

"Hey, just give me a minute, Vince," said Radmanovich with a playful smirk. He stepped to one said and unbuttoned his pants. "I gotta mark my territory before I go. I hear tell Carson's got a pretty young daughter soon coming of age," he grinned and began watering the ground at his feet. "I wanna let the other boys know they're gonna end up going toe to toe with me if they dare venture into my territory."

"Yeah, Aaron, nobody's gonna mess with a stud like you," said Boe sarcastically. "Now shove that diseased little puppy back in your pants, fall in, and let's get goin'."

Von Toth, still sitting, looked around at the men in the detail. Straub was within three feet of Boe. Georg Dreschler was on the edge of the group, standing with his arms folded across his chest. Karl Weber was rising from where he had been sitting near the edge of the bluff, and Amos Dreibach, his face tense, was looking at Von Toth as though waiting for something.

As Boe turned, he didn't see it coming.

Von Toth, abruptly up off the boulder, grabbed Radmanovich by the neck with one hand and twisted his head with the other. At the same instant, Straub came barreling for Boe and caught his neck in one great hand.

Boe by instinct lurched toward Straub, feet sliding on the wet grass; he broke Straub's hold and threw him back. But Straub struck back, catching Boe's hand with his army .45 half-drawn, knocking the gun sliding a dozen feet away while his huge hand again closed on Boe's neck. Boe grabbed Straub's hair, dragged him to the ground, and jabbed his thumbs into Straub's eyes.

The beefy, big-boned Straub instantly relinquished his hold to save his eyes, and then grabbed Boe, and face to face, they went rolling and tossing across the ground like primal beasts, gouging, ripping, and tearing.

On his back now, his heart hammering with horror, Boe's eyes locked for an instant on Von Toth's, asking why. Why have you done this?…how could you betray me? The colonel's eyes were empty and cold.

Boe, his hands savagely raked and bleeding, threw Straub off, regained his feet, and, grabbing Straub, pulled him up with him. Suddenly Straub's knee came up into his groin, and Boe's world dissolved in pain. But he swung a savage backhand across Straub's face, splitting the big man's lower lip wide, so that Boe's hand was now slick with Straub's blood.

Breathing heavily, his lungs aching, he looked at Straub as he stood circling, arms spread wide. Straub's right eye was cut and closed, his face a bloody rag, when Boe lashed out with a pulverizing blow to the jaw that dropped Straub to his knees.

Instantly, Boe turned toward Von Toth—turned just in time to see the colonel swing a stone the size of two big fists into his face. And when it hit, Boe's world was gone.

Suddenly, except for the call of birds and Straub's heavy breathing as he gazed through his blood at Von Toth, all was silent.

Von Toth looked back at his big sergeant with a steely gaze of displeasure, a scolding glare worse than the harshest words. Then Von Toth stooped and slipped the black ribbon and Iron Cross from the dead Boe's neck.

With a smirk of triumph, he looked around, exchanging glances with his men. Amos Dreibach was first on one foot and then on the other, obviously eager to move out. Karl Weber's face was relaxed. Georg Dreschler was standing exactly where he had been before, arms still across his chest, but his face was red and he was worrying his lower lip with his teeth.

Georg was gazing back at him, watching Von Toth's smirk break gradually into a barely restrained celebratory beam. Loathing Von Toth even more than before, Georg looked down on the two dead men. *Now,* he thought, *God help us, the die is cast!*

"Gentlemen," Von Toth said, "we have burned our bridges. There is no turning back. Our destination is Mexico, and from there we will go on to our glorious Fatherland to continue the fight! Hide these bodies well." He looked again at Georg. "Georg, we will need these brave men's uniforms. You and I will take on the roles of our departed overseers."

Georg paused before he spoke. His tone was restrained. "Yes, my colonel," he said, "but just how do we gain the Mexican border…sir?"

Von Toth stepped to the edge of the bluff and looked down on the Carson Ranch resting placidly in the distance. His voice utterly void of tone, he replied, "Jack Carson, Georg. Jack Carson will be our ticket to Mexico."

4

Jack Carson had seen his share of shot-up bears in his day, but never one this bullet-riddled. A mid-morning warmth settled upon the land as Jack and his eighteen-year-old son, Wade, sliced carefully through the bear's skin and began to peel it back. The walking textbook of the wilderness way that he was, Jack knew he was looked upon with utmost admiration. And he was proud of young Wade who wasn't all that far behind his dad in wilderness savvy; he knew the boy would soon enough develop the charisma and the unquestioned reverence afforded men like Jack Carson.

Jack could scarcely contain his laughter. "You boys musta thought you was in some confounded carnival the way you plugged away at this old boy."

The dead bear was hanging head-down from the sturdy limb of a ponderosa, suspended by his spread hind, and drawn up so Jack could bleed him out and begin stripping off the hide. This was a black bear, big and old—a male. The dark hair glistened in the sun, and a faint breeze parted it so the thicker fur showed underneath.

"Heck, Jack, if he'd a just dropped on the first couple of shots, this wouldn't of happened," replied John Cullum, the hunting party's leader and chief culprit in the firing free-for-all.

Jack paused with the bloody knife in his hand and looked at Cullum. "I'll let you fellas in on something just for another time," he said. "After the first couple of shots, he weren't exactly gonna go very far on you. But if this fella had been a *grizzly*—now that would'a been a different story." He grinned. "But you don't need to worry about that. The last grizzly was shot in this country more than sixty years ago."

"I'm curious, Jack. We're not on a bird hunt, so why'd you bring that cannon there?" Tom McDonald, a free-spirited, devil-may-care friend of John's, nodded toward the sleek double-barreled scattergun Jack had laid on a blanket atop a log, its breach open and the bright brass backside of a shell shining in each chamber.

Jack looked around again. "That's just in case you fella's mess up. That's my backup gun. Loaded with double ought buck, like she is, that girl'll take down

16

anything, man or beast, that you'll ever run into. Like I said, just in case you mess up." He grinned again and turned back to his work.

"Oh…" Tom gazed at the gun for a moment, then said, "Well…anyways, we got us a beauty of a bear rug there, Jack."

"Rug? From *this* shot-up hide?" Jack kept working. "We just may be able to cut you boys out a couple of *doormats* here, but I wouldn't get my hopes up for much else."

Tom turned to John. "He's just kidding, isn't he?"

Jack looked away from his cutting, set aside the knife, removed his hat, and ran a hand through his wild, wind-blown hair. "Relax, boys. I'll sew up the bullet holes and turn this into a fine-looking bear rug for one of you. Have you cut the cards yet to see whose gonna take this old boy home?"

"Not yet," answered John, shifting his glance Tom's way. "Best go do it now and get it over with."

Tom and John turned to rejoin their companions, Reverend Keith Bixby and big Donny Ruck who sat nearby at the blazing campfire Jack had built.

Keith, a straightlaced Baptist minister, sat hunched, with an iron skillet in his hand, tending two slabs of bacon sizzling over a crackling wood fire. He was a slim-built and bespectacled God-fearing man of the cloth. His hair, like a good chunk of his sense of humor, had gone missing a few years back, but he possessed an honest concern for his fellow man and made it his business to challenge nearly every person he met with the call of Jesus Christ.

Donny, a big-bellied bookkeeper about as much at home out here as a canary in a cat show, tossed another log onto the fire and waited for his fourth slice of bacon. Donny weighed in at an extraordinary 320 pounds and counting. He'd split his new hunting overalls clear up the backside the first day out and had endured his friends' jibes ever since. Having been warned that Jack had nearly lost a hunter to a companion's gunfire a couple of years back, Donny had sought out the gaudiest pair of bright orange overalls in the state of Colorado. He sure as the dickens wasn't going to be mistaken for a bear by one of his trigger-happy buddies. He'd been blessed with a thick thatch of curly black hair, and at one time had been a handsome man; but that was twenty years and 150 pounds ago. This was his first—and most certainly his last—outdoor adventure. He didn't care much for killing bears.

Tom was an alcoholic, a chain-smoker, and a hard-living truck driver, twice divorced and now living with a girl in suburban Denver. Years of alcoholism had taken a terrible toll on him, and it showed up every day in the way he got along with people. John was his best friend in the world, and Tom had jumped at the chance to spend four days in the wilderness with him.

John, an outgoing, well-to-do businessman, was built low to the ground, but he was lean and strong as a horse. He was an investor—some say a self-made millionaire—who'd been well rewarded for his many forays into the uncertain world of high finance. A keen competitor who hated to lose at anything, he was the glue that kept this foursome together.

The hunters, all four in their midforties, had grown up in the same Denver neighborhood and had attended the same grammar school. They would've been high school buddies too, if Tom had gotten that far.

At John's prodding, the others had set aside this long weekend to hunt bear in the wilds. It was John's second trip; he'd been pretty much a spectator with Jack and four others last spring when two bears were brought down, and he'd returned, determined to bring back one of his own.

"Boys, I think you got enough wood on that fire to last half the night," John said. "You can give yourselves a break now."

"It's time, fellas," said Tom as he walked up. "Time to cut the deck to see who gets the bear."

Keith chuckled. "I'll settle for the skin."

"I'll get the cards," said Donny.

"You ain't expectin' to have a hand in this card cuttin', are you, Donny?" asked Tom. "I mean, you weren't nowheres near that animal when it went down."

John placed a hand on Tom's shoulder and said quietly, "Tom, you know what we agreed to. Regardless who brings it down, we all cut the deck to see who gets the skin."

"It ain't right, though," Tom argued. "Only those who actually shot the critter ought to be allowed to cut the deck."

"We agreed to let everybody cut the deck," said Keith with a tone of finality. "We can't go back on it now."

"Yeah, but if old lard ass there gets high card, I promise I won't be no fun to be around the rest of the day," said Tom.

"And that would be something new?" scowled Donny, handing John the cards.

"Simmer down, you two," said John. He squatted on a fireside log and began anxiously shuffling the deck. John coveted that bearskin for himself, but he was a fair-minded man and would be happy for whoever went home with it. He placed the deck on the ground and pointed at it. "Donny, why don't you go first?"

Donny obliged, bending forward as far as he was able—given his great girth—to pick a card from near the top of the stack.

"Well, we know who *isn't* going to be taking home the skin," bellowed Tom exuberantly as Donny revealed his seven of clubs.

"Keith, you're next," said John.

Keith uttered an unspoken prayer before reaching for a card. That bear rug would sure look great in his living room. A six of spades.

"Tough luck, Keither," Tom chortled as he extended his hand to offer Keith a heartless pat on the back. "Looks like it's down to you and me, Johnny boy," said Tom. "You go first."

John hesitated, then took a card from the pack. He concealed it in the palm of his hand and looked at it without a trace of emotion.

"Come on. Show us what you got!" exclaimed Tom.

John slowly exposed his three of spades.

Tom broke out in jubilation. "Read 'um and weep, boys," he said as he reached to pluck a card and turned up a six of hearts.

Donny flung his big arms high in the air in celebration and let out a huge yell.

Keith and John smiled at Donny's having bested Tom for the skin.

"I knew it," growled Tom. "I just knew this fat lump would take it home. And without never firin' a single shot! Ain't fair."

Donny reacted with swift anger. Stepping toward Tom with bared teeth and predatory eyes, he clutched his tormentor's shirt with two giant hands. "I've had enough of your name-callin'!"

John and Keith took to their feet just as Tom let loose with a right that split Donny's upper lip.

Donny had never been in a fight in his life, save for the one he'd won by half a city block when the school bully took after him one day. So now he just strengthened his grip on Tom's shirt and lifted him off the ground.

Tom grabbed Donny's bulky hunting shirt in both hands.

"Hey—*hey!* Let go of one another," coaxed Keith. "We gotta talk this out, boys."

But the menacing glaze in the men's eyes warned of mayhem to come.

"Tom, you've already had too much to drink, and the day isn't half over," added John. "Back off now, and leave the hide to Donny."

"You tell him to let go of my shirt, or I'll bury his fat ass out here in these woods," snapped Tom.

"Donny, let go of the shirt," pleaded John. "He didn't mean anything by it."

But Donny held on. "Ever since we were kids, he's made fun of my weight," said Donny, his voice breaking. "I'm not takin' anymore from this pea-brained trucker!"

"Pee or git off the pot, fat boy!" Tom shouted. "Put me down and let's start throwing 'um!".

"Hey, guys, I brought you out here to hunt bear, not fight," said Jack as he ambled toward them, cheerful as always. "Fightin'll cost you extra. Now listen up. You men take five minutes to back off and think it over, and if you still wanna dance after that, then I'm all for it. But not here. This fighting by the fire'll get you burnt. There's a clearing a ways off. Now, whadya say? Five minutes?"

Donny set Tom down, and Tom loosened his grip and backed away.

"Smart move, husky," snarled Tom with a blistering glare as he stepped back. His hands were balled into fists. "You'd have come out second best, I promise you that."

"Tom, it's over. Take a walk," said John. "And no more whiskey till nightfall, you hear?"

"Back off!" spat Tom as he focused on the man who was his best friend in the world. "*All* of you, back off! The only reason you ain't glassy-eyed yourself, Johnny boy, is on account of your preacher buddy here. Should I tell him? Should I tell him what you're really like when you're out with your drinkin' buddies?"

"Nobody wants to hear anything more from you, Tom," said Keith. "Now take John's advice and walk it off."

Tom offered a mock salute, spat on the ground, and sauntered off among the trees.

5

Light rain was falling as Josh Carson finished pitching hay to mothers who were tending their newborn calves in the birthing corral. Josh's beloved German shepherd, Sarge, was nearby, now sniffing at the hay that fell from Josh's fork, now lying down and looking up at him, watching him work. The wide corrals dominated the area near the barn. Beyond the corrals, out and away, stretched the high mountain meadows that nearly four hundred head of cattle and thirty-odd fine-bred horses called home.

Amid giant blue spruce trees that stood like kings, affording shade in the summer and shelter in the winter, and against a magnificent mountain backdrop, stood the gorgeous white house with its dormers and slate gray roof. With a white picket fence setting the house off from the meadows, the picture could have adorned a June calendar. The grounds were immaculate—not a blade of grass out of place, not a weed in sight. A place of peace and order within a vast, soaring wilderness.

Stately trees lined the long, winding road leading to the ranch. Down from the house stood a hen house with no hens, a pig barn with no pigs, and a big, hundred-year-old red barn bursting with bright yellow hay. A pickup truck and a car, each new and bearing Colorado tags, were parked out near the barn; each belonged to a member of the hunting party Josh's dad, Jack Carson, had led out three days ago.

The ranch was a short horseback ride from Segundo, Colorado, some eight miles from Camp Trinidad.

Sixteen-year-old Josh Carson and his fifteen-year-old sister, Cassie, would soon mount up and be off to school in Segundo. On cold winter days, a ranch hand or their father would drive them in, but they preferred horseback.

Like their brother Wade, Josh and Cassie idolized their father and sorely missed their mother who had been taken by cancer just over four years ago.

Jack Carson considered it a personal favor that the good Lord had answered his prayers and granted Cassie her mother's comely features: a curvaceous build; silky, soft, chestnut-colored skin; misty blue eyes; and straight blond hair with a mingling of brown. And the winsome smile on her pretty face rivaled any he had ever seen.

Josh was slim and a tad cocky, not yet filled out like Wade or his dad and not yet stretched to their six-foot-something height.

Josh and Cassie held down full-time jobs at the ranch and went to school on the side. Josh claimed that the only reason he attended school was to eat his lunch, and if you ever got a look at his lunch, you'd know what he meant. To call the work they did at the ranch "a job" was a misnomer. "Hobby" would be a better word. They so loved working with the animals and caring for the grounds that neither was apt to venture far from this place when they reached adulthood.

As for schooling, Cassie had come away with the lion's share of aptitude. But the boys were smart in their own way: "nature smart," their dad called it.

Joe and Hilda Koivunen were the hired help at the Carson Ranch. They'd lived here over thirty years. Hilda earned her keep in the ranch house itself, cooking, cleaning, and generally looking after the family. Joe was the ranch hand in charge of minding the cattle and horses and keeping the grounds in immaculate condition. German immigrants, the Koivunens had found a home in Colorado and had lived at the ranch from the start, working for Jack's folks before they had passed on. Joe and Hilda had helped raise young Jack since he was twelve. They'd become much more than hired help to the Carsons. They were family.

Joe, a cadaverous man with skeletal arms and high, hollow cheeks, had suffered a devastating injury years ago while helping break a wild bronco. Tossed off the back end, he'd met up with one of its hooves on the way down, landing him in the hospital with a concussion. Had the blow struck him an inch higher, he'd surely have died. When he awoke, he discovered he'd been blinded in his left eye, and that it would take many hours of reconstructive surgery to put his face back together. His speech was still a bit slurred and his face disfigured, but he had never lost his love for horses.

Hilda was a thickset, buxom woman with a heart as big as all of Colorado. Her hair in a bun, she wore a huge gingham apron over an ankle-length dress.

The Koivunens held a lifetime lease on their home, a little house built a hundred years ago as the first ranch house, and now stood to the west beyond the picket fence. Here they would live until their dying day.

With a delightful spring day in the making, golden sunbeams and a fresh breeze poured in through the kitchen window of the big new house while fresh-baked bread sat cooling on the counter.

"Joshua, you're gonna be late for school," called Hilda from the kitchen window.

"I'm coming," Josh called back in his typically buoyant tone.

Cassie sat at the breakfast table studying for a spelling test; she picked lightly at her scrambled eggs and toast, as though they were implanted in chicken manure.

"You eat up, young lady," bossed Hilda.

"I'm just not hungry, auntie," she replied.

"You're never hungry. Now eat."

Cassie took a bite of toast to appease her overseer. "You never bug Josh about eating. It's not fair."

"Your brudder doesn't need any bugging. He'd eat da tableclot' if I let him. Gets it from his dad and his dad before him. Never met a Carson male you had to beg to eat."

"He doesn't eat much breakfast, though."

"Child, Josh is like doze cows grazing out in da field. He eats all day long. It's you I'm worried about." Hilda sensed a heartache in Cassie, and so she sat down next to her, reaching to toss back a wayward strand of blond hair from the youngster's face.

"You got boys on da brain, don't you, child?"

Cassie went a bit red—she blushed easily—and looked up as though she'd been accused of theft. "Boys? I'm too young for boys, auntie. At least, Daddy says I am."

"I don't know if it's possible to be too young for boys, my dear. It's like being too young for ice cream or chocolate cake. It's yust a natural t'ing. I was married to your uncle Joe at seventeen. Had it to do over again, I'd do yust dat." Hilda lifted a loving hand to Cassie's left cheek. "You yust be sure to guard your heart and never, never do anyt'ing you'd live to regret. You hear?"

Cassie smiled and put her hand on Hilda's. "I hear, auntie. Don't you worry about me." She glanced up at the kitchen clock. "I gotta run up to my room and get my math book before I go."

Hilda stood up and reached for a small paper sack on the counter and handed it to Cassie. "Here's your lunch, and you eat it—you hear?"

Cassie pecked at Hilda's cheek. "I will, auntie." And she turned and ran up the stairs.

With the glow of unblemished youth, Josh swung open the front door and made for the kitchen. "I'm starving, auntie. What you got?"

Hilda headed back to the kitchen, reached for a dinner plate, and threw the rest of the scrambled eggs on it. "If you'd take da time to eat before you do da chores, I could keep it warm and fresh for you."

"No time," he answered as he shoveled the eggs into his mouth, not bothering to sit. "Can't be late for school!" He reached for Cassie's plate and wolfed down her nearly untouched eggs, some tumbling out the corners of his mouth.

"Did anyone ever tell you dat's bad for your digestion, young man?" scolded Hilda. She said this with her hands on her hips and a disapproving frown on her face.

"Hmm...got no time for digesting my food. Can't be late again today. Old Missus Turner's taking to have me write lines on the board for being late. See you!"

As he hurried by, Hilda kissed his cheek and handed him his lunch—six ham-and-lettuce sandwiches, four cookies, a banana, and a twelve-ounce container of canned peaches. "Now don't forget your homework. You did do your homework last night, didn't you?" she asked as she followed him to the door.

"Well, I...I...come on, auntie, you know how busy I've been with the calving!"

"Joshua Carson," she reached out to gently pinch his ear, "I'm going to be hearing from Mrs. Turner again. So help me, I'll rope you to da dining room table and force feed you your homework if dat woman gets after me again."

"I'll work on it at recess. I promise."

"If your mudder were alive, young man, she'd turn you upside down and give you da what-for on account of your idleness. I'm yust too soft on you."

"Love you, auntie," Josh said as he bent to affectionately kiss her forehead. Then he hustled out the front door.

6

Joe Koivunen was on his way inside for a second cup of coffee when Sarge's deep-throated snarl alerted him to a pair of American soldiers escorting men in POW garb marching up the path.

Josh and Cassie had just come out onto the front porch on their way to school, and Hilda was standing in the doorway. Like Joe, they wondered just what two American guards and a dozen prisoners of war were doing so far off the main highway linking the Segundo mines to Camp Trinidad. They'd seen these work details out on the highway leading to the mines, but what were they doing here?

Sarge dutifully sprang from the porch and ran out to confront the visitors, growling low in his throat, the gray hackles along his spine raised.

The American guard in charge ordered a halt, sank to one knee, and extended the back of his hand to Sarge to sniff.

Joe watched Sarge warily approach the man in the corporal's uniform, examine the hand with his nose, then, hackles still raised, lower his tail, and still growling, back away. As Sarge came back to him, Joe looked down at him. "Sarge, vot in da verld?" He looked back at the guard who had just risen from his knee and was standing looking around at the yard.

Puzzled, Joe said, "I beg yer pardon, sir. I ain't never seen dat dog do dat before." He paused, "You men are a long vays from home, ain't you?"

"You're telling me," the guard said with a pleasant laugh. "My first time leading a crew to the Segundo Mines, and I seem to have taken a wrong turn. My captain's gonna have my stripes for this."

"Da mines is straight back da vay you come," said Joe, his finger pointing due north. "Yust go back to da highvay, and turn to da left. Da mines is due vest about t'ree miles."

"Ah, so I just should'a kept on going west on the highway then!" said the guard. He removed his cap and ran a hand through his short-cut hair.

"Dat's it," said Joe. "You come about'n hour off yer course."

The guard appeared to hesitate. "Say," he said, "you folks couldn't spare a cold drink, could you? That sun's burning pretty hot this morning."

Cassie reached to swing open the screen door, saying, "Come on in. We've got orange juice in the ice box."

"Thank you, darling," said the guard. "Sorry to trouble you." He turned and addressed the other guard, a slender young man with black hair and light blue eyes. "Keep a close eye on these Krauts," he said, and then, "You men, at ease. Get out of the sun and rest in the shade of that tree."

"D'ere's a hand pump d'ere," Joe called to the prisoners. "Drink yer fill."

The corporal turned to Joe and smiled. "Thank you, sir," he said, then he turned, and following Cassie and Josh, in a moment, was inside the house.

Joe said to the blue-eyed guard, "Can't understand how you men could get yerselves so lost out here! You must *all* be on your first trip to da mines."

"Yes, sir," the young man replied. "We're green as grass. New batch of prisoners. New guards."

Joe laughed. "Da blind leading da blind."

"Yes, sir," answered the guard with a broad smile that made Joe instantly like him.

"You OK, son? Yer face is a little flush. Da sun too hot fer ya? Are ya sick?"

Georg Dreschler hesitantly raised his eyes, and when he did, they locked with the old man's. Georg's insides trembled. He was fiercely agitated by Von Toth's audacious plan, but he was in bitter, angry shock over the murders. Von Toth had told them of the plan only this morning after breakfast. No chance to say yes or no. The colonel hadn't asked for volunteers; he had issued orders. The rules of war said it was the duty of every prisoner of war to try to escape, but this? My *God*, not *this*! Georg gazed into the old man's kind eyes with the desperate hope that these people were not next in line. The old man's voice broke into his thoughts.

"Can I get you a drink?" asked Joe.

"No. No thank you, sir. I'm OK." Trying to smile, he looked around nervously. "This is *truly* a magnificent ranch."

"Ya, ve like it here," said Joe with a contented grin. He nodded toward one of the men, a big man with a lower lip fiercely swollen and an eye bruised and shut. "So vot happened to dat fella dere?" he said. "Looks like somebody busted him bad!"

Georg smiled in spite of himself. "He got in a fight this morning," he said.

Joe laughed lightly. "An' vot does da uder fella look like?"

As the image of the dead Boe appeared in his mind, the smile faded from Georg's face. But at that moment, the boy and girl he'd just seen go in, burst back out the front door.

"We gotta run," the boy said, touching the brim of his work-worn cowboy hat to Georg as he and the girl headed for the horses tied to an old hitching rail by the nearest corral. "Cain't be late for school."

Georg nodded and smiled, relieved that they were going. The boy was mounting up, and the girl had taken the reins of her horse, when Von Toth stepped out on the porch. Georg's breath caught in his throat when he heard the colonel call to them.

"So, where're you off to in such a hurry?" the colonel asked, and he took another sip from his glass of juice.

Georg Dreschler watched, tense and afraid.

"To school," answered the girl as she reached up for the saddle horn.

"Yeah, we cain't be late again today, or I'll be up you-know-what crick without a paddle," said the boy. "Have yourselves a good day."

"We'll do that," said Von Toth. "Say, might I inquire of you? This wouldn't be the Carson Ranch I've heard so much about, would it?"

"Why, yeah, it is," said the boy. A proud boyish beam broke across his face. "I'm Josh Carson and this is my sister, Cassie."

"Wonderful! A family operation! It's even better than they described it. But where are all the ranch hands? You can't possibly run a place like this without help."

Georg winced, thinking, *For God's sake, don't tell him!*

"You're looking at the ranch hands, sir," said Cassie. "Our pa and older brother are the only other ones, and they're off hunting bear."

"You don't say! By the looks of these vehicles, I would guess it to be a sizeable hunting party."

It was Joe who answered. "Nah," he said. "Yust four good ol' boys from Denver out for a long veekend in da mountains."

Hilda's high-pitched voice echoed from the back of the house. "Sarge, here boy!"

"Your mother?" Von Toth asked as the dog bolted toward the house.

"Heck no," answered Josh. "She only *thinks* she's our mother. That's Uncle Joe's wife, Aunt Hilda."

"Our mother passed on," added Cassie.

"I'm so sorry to hear that. Another thing—I'm told there's a pass leading to New Mexico not far from here," said Von Toth.

Josh pointed to the high country. "Raton Pass, about a day's ride southeast. Prettiest country you'll ever live to see."

"Ah, a likely spot for your father's hunting party."

"No, they're about as far from Raton Pass as you can get, actually not far from the mines you men are headed to." Josh gently dug his heels into his mount to ride out. "Uncle Joe here'll fill you in on anything else you need to know. We gotta get to school."

Abruptly, Von Toth ended the façade. Tossing aside his glass and drawing his pistol, he dropped the Southern drawl, and in a rock-hard tone, said, "Get down off your horses and tie them up. You won't be attending school today, children."

Cassie and Josh reined in and stared at the man. What was going on here? An American soldier drawing on them and threatening them at gunpoint?

"Haf' you gone off your nut, Corporal?" inquired an astonished Joe.

Georg was hardly breathing now, hoping to God Von Toth would have compassion on these people.

"I said, get off your horses now, and I won't ask a third time. Georg, help them down."

Georg reluctantly crossed to where the horses stood with their dumbfounded riders and took the reins of both horses. "Please get down," Georg said, making eye contact with the girl—Cassie—hoping she would see kindness there. Josh and Cassie slowly dismounted.

The "corporal" turned to Joe. "Off my nut?" he said. "I'm afraid not, Joe." He waved the muzzle of the pistol toward the house. "If you'll all just come inside, I'll do my best to explain the predicament you find yourselves in. Georg, you and the children join us, and have your pistol ready."

Georg drew the pistol, the weight of his reluctance making it hard to hold.

Joe's stride stiffened. As he climbed the porch steps, the light of understanding broke upon his mind. "You men are POWs from Camp Trinidad," he said quietly.

"There you go," answered the colonel. "You catch on fast. Colonel Helmet Von Toth of the German *Wehrmacht*. Now I'm hoping you all are of a cooperative mind today, so no one gets hurt."

Cassie came up beside Joe and put one arm around the old man's waist. "What do you *want* with us?" She projected anger through her eyes and felt fear pulling down at the corners of her mouth.

"What we want, young lady, is some food, horses, and clothing. We'll be on our way soon. All you need, my dear, is to follow my simple orders." Holding the door open, he motioned with the pistol. "Go on in."

Inside, Georg's eyes fell with fascination upon the mounted hunting trophies on the wall, and the mammoth grizzly bear rug on the hardwood living room floor. A big box of fresh-cut firewood lay next to a massive brick fireplace that dominated the adjoining family room. The place was as impressive inside as it was out.

"You're making a break for Mexico?" Josh said. His voice trembled with anger.

"Very perceptive, young man. And that's where the horses come in," added Von Toth as he settled on the arm of a big recliner. His voice grew soft and persuasive. "We'd never make it out of this country if we took to the highways." Again he motioned with the pistol. "Now…let's call 'Aunt Hilda' into the room, and we can give everybody their jobs for the morning."

Aunt Hilda didn't need to be called. She came out of the laundry room to investigate the voices, wiping wet hands on her apron. "Vut is it? Children, vy aren't you on your vay to school?"

Von Toth replied, "There's been a change of plan, Aunt Hilda. May I call you that?"

Hilda never answered. The two drawn handguns set her mind instantly abuzz with alarm.

Joe strolled over, put his arm around her and drew her to him. "Dey're escaped prisoners of war, dear. It vill be all right. Yust do as dey say."

"Well put, Joe," said Von Toth with a smile. "That wouldn't be a German accent I detect, would it?"

Joe answered, "It iss. Ve came here from Hamburg many years ago."

"Splendid," said Von Toth. "I'm from Prussia. I believe one of my men outside is from Hamburg. Now, what do you say to our getting to work so that you can get us off your hands? Hilda, I'm putting you and the young lady here in charge of packing food for our weeklong journey to the Mexican border. Sandwiches for today, canned goods for the duration, and plenty to drink. Put in first-aid supplies and whatever else you think might make our difficult journey more agreeable. I'm sure you're used to packing for hunting parties out here. Don't disappoint me. Georg, you stay inside and keep them working. Never let them out of your sight. You men will come with me and help saddle some horses. Understood?"

"Yes, sir," said Joe as they made for the door.

"You'll let us be when we've done as you ask?" inquired Josh.

"You have my word as an officer and a gentleman," answered Von Toth. "Just help get those horses saddled, and we'll be on our way. So tell me, young man, when can we expect your father back?"

"Late afternoon, early evening." Josh's eyes narrowed with suspicion. "Why? What's my dad got to do with this?"

"Just curious, young man. Just curious."

◆   ◆   ◆

Josh and Joe worked feverishly to saddle the horses.

Von Toth stood with pistol ready to deal out death to his captives should they try to play the hero. He looked toward the men lounging beneath the tree. "Sergeant Straub, come over here."

Straub came and stood at attention before him.

"Sergeant, I want you to take a couple of men and go search the house for firearms. Bring every gun you find out here and distribute them to the men." He paused, thinking. "And clothes. Find clothes that won't call attention to us."

◆   ◆   ◆

As Hilda and Cassie packed the saddlebags with food, Cassie's eye went often to their young German guard. "Georg," had she heard them call him that? He seemed so out of place in all this. He lacked the hardness, the do-or-die determination it took to draw a gun on innocent people.

Georg noticed her glances. *Such a beautiful, innocent girl,* he thought. Dear God! He wished for nothing more than to make all this go away! He wasn't a *soldier*! He'd have gladly sat out the war at Camp Trinidad—away from the killing and suffering back home!…and away from the killing here. As for this day's adventure, Georg Dreschler felt he had betrayed everything he held dear.

7

"A delicious lunch, Hilda," said Von Toth after his second ham sandwich. "We are forever indebted to you."

"Yes. Excellent," added Georg, his voice quiet and gracious.

Hilda narrowed her eyes in contempt and refused to lift her staring gaze from the table. But at last she glanced up to see the big sergeant, "Straub," she thought they called him, sitting in silence, his split lips set in a permanent scowl. He was breaking off bits of meat and bread and gingerly placing them in his swollen mouth. His two lower teeth bent and broken, and she wondered if that deformed-looking jaw was shattered. She thought it probably was, and probably from some beating he had taken when these men subdued their guards. She wondered about those men—if they were dead, just as she was wondering if she and Joe and the children would soon be dead.

The others were outside resting under a tree, eating their sandwiches and keeping close watch in case Jack's party returned ahead of time.

"So tell me, Joe—you folks must miss our beloved Fatherland a great deal?"

It was the colonel, whose voice Hilda had already learned to hate.

Joe cleared his throat before answering. "Ve vent back for a visit in t'irty-t'ree, but ve have no desire to ever go back again."

"Ve have no use for your Hitler!" spat Hilda and gave him the most withering glare she could muster. "He's a madman! Ve pray every day for his overt'row." The sound of her own voice startled her; these were the first words she'd spoken to their captors since their abduction.

She saw Von Toth glance over his shoulder and lift a finger to his mouth.

He whispered, "To be honest with you, some of us aren't terribly fond of the little tyrant ourselves." He leaned back with a smug curl on his lips and raised his voice. "My allegiance is to Germany, and rest assured I'll fight to my last breath to protect her from her enemies! My father fought in the Great War, my grandfather in the Prussian War, and my great-grandfather against Napoleon. I come from a long line of warriors. We don't give up without a fight."

"How is it you let them take you prisoner then," asked Josh, "if you was gonna fight to the last breath?"

"I assure you that I had no say in my being taken prisoner, my young friend. I had been hospitalized, thoroughly incapacitated by an aerial attack the previous week, badly broken inside and out. One of your P-47s scored a direct hit on my Panther during our defense of Tunis. I lay unconscious in my burning tank." He paused to place a hand on Sergeant Straub's shoulder. "I surely would have been incinerated had Sergeant Straub not risked his life to heroically pull me from the wreckage. When your armies overran our base, I was shipped off to your Camp Trinidad, and I've spent these last months recuperating from my injuries and planning for this very day when we'd gain our freedom and begin the journey back to defend our homeland." He straightened and pushed his chair back. "Now, we must be on our way. Would you mind seeing us off at the stable?"

Anxiety darkened the faces of the Koivunens, Josh, and Cassie as they reluctantly led the POWs out the front door.

At the stables, they found thirteen horses saddled, another four loaded with supplies, and three more tied to pack horses in reserve.

Each of the POWs was now decked out in a flannel shirt, faded Levis, and scuffed boots, all pilfered from the ranch closets. One or two had found a long canvas duster split up the back for riding, and some wore spurs. Everyone wore a hat, most, sweat-stained and dirty.

Von Toth looked at his captives. He needed a guide through Raton Pass. The youngsters, Josh and Cassie, would do nicely. Old Joe knew the area, but the young ones would make better pawns if he needed to barter their way out of a tight spot.

"And now for my surprise," said Von Toth, with what he hoped was an intimidating smile. "We are in need of guides to see us through Raton Pass and on into New Mexico." He looked directly at Josh and Cassie. "You young people will oblige us. No?"

"You want us to guide you in your escape?" asked Josh. The thought of helping these men revolted him.

"Yes. Yes, you know the way. Think of it as a field trip from school. You'll be back home safe and sound in a day or two."

"Take me instead," said Joe. "I know da vay as vell as dey do."

"No, I considered that, Joe. Thank you anyway. I'll take the young people."

"So vut you really vant is hostages, not guides," Joe shouted, fixing Von Toth face to face.

Von Toth was growing angry. "Georg, take the Koivunens into the stable. I'll be in shortly."

Georg took Hilda's arm gently, but she resisted, and he tightened his grip and forced her. Hilda's eyes were moist with tears as he jostled her and Joe.

Cassie called after her in a pleading, anxious voice, "It'll be all right, auntie. He won't hurt us!"

Joe bunched his fists and growled. "You harm dese children, Von Tot', and dere fodder vill track you to da gates of hell."

In a flush of hot anger, Josh stepped toward Von Toth. "You gave me your word you'd let us be once we saddled up the horses and fed you!"

"Young man, you must understand that our countries are at war, and I've had a change of heart."

Infuriated, Josh narrowed his eyes. "I'll tell you this much, Colonel, we ain't leaving with you till I see my aunt and uncle driving off outta here safe and sound."

"I tink da colonel has udder plans for us," said Joe quietly as he turned back to face them from the stable door.

"Whadya *mean?*" exclaimed Cassie, her face glazed with shock. "*What* other plans?"

Reacting to a scowling glare from Von Toth, Georg forced the old couple into the stable.

Von Toth cast a terrifying look at Josh, drew his pistol, and aimed it at Cassie's forehead. "Now, what was that about your not being willing to leave here? *You*, young man, are in no position to dictate terms to me. I will kill you both right here and now. You'll see us through that pass and on into New Mexico, or I'll blow your brains out. Do you hear?" He paused for effect and softened his voice. "What a sight that would be for Daddy to come home to tonight! I do hope you'll reconsider your audacious demand while I go have a word with the Koivunens." He reverted to German and ordered Straub to keep a close eye on them.

Josh watched Straub lever a cartridge into the chamber of one of the .30-30s stolen from the house, and then level it at him. He had never looked down the muzzle of a loaded gun before. He looked up at Straub's swollen, bruised, war-hardened face and wondered about the man behind it.

Cassie watched Von Toth enter the stable and, in a rush of terror, she fell into her brother's arms, screaming and weeping.

Josh felt a terrible chill—a horror; the butcher's ax was about to fall and he was powerless to do anything about it.

Two pistol shots shattered the stillness.

Josh and Cassie, ignoring Sergeant Straub's steel-plated Germanic cry to stand fast or die, rushed into the stable. Their eyes widened as the sunlight slicing in through cracks in the barn walls fell across Hilda and Joe lying still on the bloody straw.

The steely-eyed German officer met them at the door. Cold-blooded murder coming as naturally to him as the breath he drew, he said, "Dead people don't talk. Yes, look. Take a good look, children. Do you still want to negotiate with me?"

Josh and Cassie gazed transfixed. Gripped with horror, Cassie collapsed into her brother's arms, and Josh gawked in disbelief. It was their first taste of humanity's truly dark side.

Through a fog of confused anguish, he heard Von Toth barking at Straub to collect their horses, and then realized he was now talking to him and Cassie. "You will understand all this one day. Casualties such as these are a natural consequence of war."

Tears were running down Josh's face now. His heart was breaking and his voice cracked as he said, "Casualties? These people were not at war. They wouldn't have done you no harm. You could'a brung 'um along or just tied 'um up. What kind of a man are you?"

"A determined man, Josh. A very desperate and determined man, and I cannot leave behind any loose ends. Do you see now what will become of you if you refuse to cooperate? Now, let's go before your father returns. If you will simply agree to see us through Raton Pass, you'll be back here by tomorrow."

"You gave me your word once before, Colonel," said Josh as he led Cassie out the door, hate and sorrow churning in his heart. "Don't go pissin' down my back and tell me it's raining out!"

Colonel Von Toth ignored the boy. He was thinking of one more thing: Jack Carson, the legendary mountain man. With him alive, the plan was in jeopardy. He took aside Sergeant Straub. "You pick out three men," he said to Straub, "and set an ambush here for Jack Carson and his hunting party. They'll be along before nightfall. Not one of them can escape. Do you understand?"

"Yes, my colonel. We will kill them all."

Then with anger, "You've disappointed me once today, Sergeant. Don't do it again. Clear?"

"Clear, sir."

"Good. Once you've killed them, hide their bodies here in the stable and catch up to us. And bring another four fresh mounts for yourselves." He pointed in the direction of Raton Pass. "Ride to the southeast. Watch for tracks. At sundown we'll set up camp and fire one shot every hour on the hour so that you can find us."

"We'll find you, sir."

Von Toth patted his arm. "Good. I'm counting on you, Sergeant."

◆   ◆   ◆

They were a half-mile out when Josh, noticing that the big man with the beat-up face was not with them, reined in beside Von Toth to confront him. "Colonel, you're missing some men. Where are they?"

"Sergeant Straub was feeling ill; they'll be along as soon as he feels well enough to ride."

"You're lying again. You left those men back there to kill my pa."

Von Toth brought the party to a standstill. He gazed at the ground before him, removed the Stetson he'd stolen to run a hand over his brush-cut hair and spoke slowly, tonelessly. "Put yourself in my place, Josh. What would *you* have done? Left a man like your father alive to track us down?"

Cassie, sick with fear, her face wet with tears, shouted in a voice high and hysterical, "My brother wouldn't kill defenseless old folks and somebody's daddy just to save his own skin!"

Josh defied Von Toth with a bitter stare. "We ain't going! Not unless you send word to those men to come join us—now!"

Josh stared at Von Toth's black expression and watched as the officer drew his stolen pistol, cocked it, and pointed it again at Cassie's head. "There you go negotiating with me again. We've been over this before. Well, we'll just have to find that pass without you."

"No!" pleaded Cassie, strangled by fear and tears.

Josh looked on in horror and disgust. "OK, let her be!" he said. "We'll go with you now!" He took a deep breath to control his emotions and said, "I always wondered what kind of man it took to commit cold-blooded murder. Now I know."

Von Toth fixed Josh with glistening, evil black eyes, and his tone was final. "This is the second time you've defied me. Once more will mean instant death for both of you. No warning. Is that clear?"

Desolate but stoic, Joshua Carson nodded his compliance. They were, he thought, sheep on their way to the slaughterhouse. No rights, no options. Do or die. This was a glimpse of hell itself.

"I shouldn't worry so," said Von Toth, looking up and gazing disarmingly at the vast blue expanse overhead. "You said you are expecting your father by early this evening. I've instructed my men to give up their vigil at the dinner hour and then ride to join us. You must pray that your father arrives sometime after that. By then we'll be too far along for him to be of any concern to us."

In a spasm of rage, Josh swung his horse around. "Colonel, my pa says there's a kind of man that if his lips are movin' you know he's lyin'. I see now that you're that kind'a man."

8

It was well past noon when Jack and Wade finished up skinning the bear. They had intended to make do with a light lunch and then push on to the ranch before supper, but the hunters insisted on one more of Jack's fabulous steak feasts before moving on.

Jack told John and Wade to wrap young potatoes for the fire pit.

"I swear I'm so hungry I could eat the rear end out of a skunk," said John.

"Now that beats any hunger I've ever known," replied Wade with a throaty chuckle.

"So, your pa tells me you're off to fight the Japs next month, huh?" asked John.

"Yep. Going to San Francisco to join the navy. Figured I'd sit this'n out, but old Uncle Sam couldn't seem to get the job done without me."

"Ah, a draftee?"

"Yeah. I figured if I gotta fight, I may as well choose the navy. I always wanted to see the world. I figure the navy's the best way to do it."

For a while, they wrapped potatoes in silence.

"So tell me about your dad," said John. "After your mama passed on, he never found anyone else?"

"No. Dad said he'd never find another one like her, so why settle for second best."

"Yeah. I hear your mom was a beautiful woman."

"Beautiful inside and out. Her passing left a huge hole in our hearts, especially Dad's."

"He really loved her, didn't he."

"Oh yeah. Dad even gave up his chewing habit when he met her, but he took it up again after she'd passed. If she'd told him to give up eating, he'd a died of starvation just to please her."

"Even with her gone, he seems happy."

"I think you'd have to hack off all four limbs to take my dad's smile away, and then only maybe."

At that moment, Jack turned from among the trees, tightening his belt, and tossed a roll of toilet paper and a bar of soap into his backpack. "I swear," he said, "that has to be the most underrated experience known to man." A broad, toothy grin lighted his face. "My rectum's still a tingling."

"Jack," Tom said, drawing on a cigarette, "if taking a dump is the best feeling you've had lately, I suggest you start dating again." Tom's newborn Western twang was typical of hunters after four days with superdrawlers like Jack and Wade.

"You boys can laugh all you want, but the good Lord just seems to bless some folk with the ability to enjoy certain things more than others."

John broke in. "I hate to change this important topic, but when we gonna chuck these steaks on the grill? I swear I could eat a horse right now."

"Patience, my friend," said Jack. "Let the taters cook a bit more."

Keith joined Jack on a log by the fire, scratched his heavily bristled face, and asked, "So when do we get to hear your mountain lion story, Jack?"

Jack snorted. "Which one?"

"Come on," said Keith. "You promised to tell us about the one that near bit your head off."

"Oh, that one," he replied sarcastically, staring off into the jagged landscape. Jack unfastened the top button of his shirt, pealed back the left collar, and turned to expose a sizeable lion's-tooth scar. "This old boy'd been stealing cattle from us all winter afore I got up the gumption to hunt him. I went after him alone with my hunting dogs. He bushwhacked me not far from here one Sunday mornin'. Knocked me clean off my horse. Never seen him coming. Next thing I knew, I was rolling around on the ground with this old boy biting and clawing at me. I'd be dead if it weren't for my dogs. They lit into that darned cat and distracted him just enough for me to draw this old hunting knife. Stuck him three times afore he ran off and bled to death about a mile downhill."

Young Wade looked on his dad with reverence; all he wanted in this world was to be another Jack Carson; a man who could square his shoulders and look on life with courage and savvy.

"Jack, you ought to write a book about your experiences," said Tom.

"Long as he promised to leave out the glowing over his bowel movements, I'd buy a copy," said Wade.

As the laughter died, Jack reached for the six steaks—each one big enough to feed a small family—and threw them on the grill.

Wade handed out plates, napkins, and utensils.

Jack's steak wasn't on the fire a minute before he stabbed at it and laid it on his plate already fat with a baked potato and carrots. From a tin cup, he sipped black coffee, drew back, and looking into the cup said, "Tastes a lot like diesel oil, wouldn't you say, boys? Reverend, I ain't waitin' for you boys to burn all the natural goodness out of your meat. You can ask God's blessing on this grub anytime your ready."

Keith smiled, removed his cap, and bowed his head.

Smart-assed Tom broke in. "Over the teeth, through the gums, look out stomach, here she comes—dig in." He was the only one laughing. He hadn't passed up a single chance to razz his old buddy Keith this entire trip, so no one was surprised at his sacrilege.

Keith followed with a short blessing on the food.

In further mockery, Tom crossed himself.

Big Donny had been silent since his run-in with Tom, but spoke up now. "So, Jack, they got some law about not shooting female bears like they do for moose and deer?"

Jack led the others in a good belly laugh and said, "Trouble is, Donny, the male bears don't grow no antlers, and darned if *I'm* gonna stroll on up and ask one of 'um to lift a leg."

John threw an arm around his blushing buddy and said, "I declare, Donny, what you lack in intelligence, you more than make up for in ignorance."

Tom gazed up serenely at the majestic mountain before him and asked, "Ever hunt mountain goat, Jack?"

"I've shot at least one of pretty near everything that takes breath in these parts," Jack answered before thrusting a forkful of carrots and potato into his wide mouth. "Except a human being, of course. Matter of fact, the only hunter I didn't bring back alive was on a mountain-goat hunt a few years back."

The others stopped eating, waiting for Jack to finish the story.

"Whadya mean, Jack? You can't just leave us in suspense. Finish the goldarn story," demanded Tom.

Jack's habitual smile took momentary leave. He took another bite of his blood-drenched steak, chewed on it, stared at the fire, wiped some blood from his chin, and started in. "This here city fella comes all the way from St. Louie to hunt mountain goat. Four other hunters and me. One of the best hunts I ever been on. Good weather. Great bunch of guys. Shot us three goats in all, including one by this here St. Louie businessman. Well, last night out, we're all sitting around a campfire, warm and happy as pigs in mud, under a big, starry sky. Everybody's drinking a little beer and carrying on. Darned if this St. Louie fella don't just get up from the fire and walk off. Couple of minutes later, we heard a rifle shot and found this old boy with his brains scattered all over the bush."

"Why...why'd he ever do such a thing?" asked Tom, a fork in one hand, a knife in the other, hands spread wide at his sides.

"We all knew he was under a lotta pressure," answered Jack, whacking a fly hovering over his plate. He took another pull at his coffee and looked pensively into the half-empty cup. "Bad marriage, business failures—he'd shared his entire life story with us on the hunt. I suspect he was having such a great time out here that he just couldn't face going back to what was waiting for him in St. Louie."

Keith stopped chewing and swallowed hard, gazed at the ground, and said, "Why, that's just plumb awful."

For a moment there was only silence, save for the hum of flies.

"Yeah, well I never promised you a happy ending, preacher," Jack responded soft and low like he was delivering a eulogy. He wiped his mouth and went back to his steak. "I know that kind of story's about as popular on a hunting trip as a truckload of dead babies in a mother's day parade. You're the first bunch I ever shared it with."

The men, now fat and happy from their mountain feast, pitched in to clean the site in preparation for the ride back to the ranch. Jack and Keith hauled the dishes to a nearby stream and washed them.

"We gotta be fairly close to the ranch, haven't we Jack?" asked Keith.

"Close as darn is to swearing. Pardon the expression. We should be back by the early evening, long as Donny doesn't hold us up again."

"I think he'll be OK today. I'm sure we can get him to ride most of the way. He just can't stand heights. Being up on a horse that's going down a steep slope freaks him out."

"I don't mind him walking his mount downhill. Heck, it actually saves wear and tear on the critter. But be switched if I'm gonna let him haul ass uphill. It's dangerous riding in the dark in this country. Lost my bearings and got stuck out here in the dark one time. Blame horse went clean out from under me, and I was airborn about twenty feet straight downhill. Would'a been crushed by that critter if he'd landed on me. No sir, we ain't riding in the dark tonight."

"Don't worry about Donny. He'll understand our need to press on. He was just brought up a little sheltered is all. I'm sure we can coax him to ride the whole way."

"Oh, we'll coax him all right. I got a two-inch rope along. We'll drag his sorry backside back to the ranch if none else."

"He's got a big heart, you know," Keith said.

"I got news for you, preacher. Donny's got a big everything."

"No, I'm serious. Know what he did this morning? He gave me the bear skin. I know he wanted it bad, but that's Donny. Give away the shirt on his back if some other fella could make better use of it."

"Well, that is kind of him. What? Did old Tom there turn it down first?" asked Jack with unbridled sarcasm.

Keith laughed. "Hmph. Those two never did get along, even as kids. But they hung out like brothers." There was a lull in the conversation as Keith considered his next question. He stopped his washing to straighten his back and glance over at Jack. He said, "Jack, I hope you don't mind my asking, but I'm curious about the spiritual side of Jack Carson."

"Oh, I don't mind you asking, preacher. Wouldn't respect you if you hadn't."

"Do you know the Lord, Jack?"

"Like the back of my hand."

"I mean, know him as your personal savior?"

"Yes, sir, I do," Jack answered as he thrust a wad of chewing tobacco into his mouth. "Don' be fooled none by my cussing and chewing and beer drinking. I've made my peace with the Almighty. I realized long ago that being a follower of Jesus Christ ain't about saying no to strong drink and attending Sunday school. God knows I love him and his dear, soul-savin' son, and I sure enough am bringing up my youngins to do just the same. There's two places you don't find no atheists in this world—in a foxhole under enemy fire and out here in God's own Rocky Mountains."

Keith patted him on the shoulder and said, "I'm glad to hear it, Jack."

As the two rejoined their companions, John drank the last of his coffee and pointed to the vintage 1800s pistol strapped to Jack's leg. "You ever wonder what that old fire iron is worth on the open market, Jack? I'd say it'd fetch a pretty price for you. And I'll bet you can't be making much money on cattle and guiding these days."

"I see you been reading my mail," Jack said with a light laugh.

"Well, how about it? Have you ever considered putting it up for sale? You told me last year you inherited it from the great Kit Carson. I suspect you could get thousands of dollars for it from some museum."

"John, my friend, there's things that money just can't buy, and this here sidearm is just such a one. I had it since I was a young'un. I'd feel naked without it."

9

The gleam in big Donny Ruck's sleep-deprived, black-circled eyes said he'd had a glimpse of heaven itself—the majestic Carson Ranch against a glorious sunset. Civilization at last!

"What time would it be, Jack?" asked Donny.

"Time to get down off these goldarn horses," groaned a saddle-sore Tom.

Jack checked his watch. "Nearing six thirty. Why'd you ask? Got a big date tonight, Donny?"

"Yeah, a date with my bathtub. I swear, I hurt in places I didn't know existed."

"Another couple of days," Jack said, "and you boys would've been broke in. It's the first three days in the saddle that's hard on you." Jack turned to address the men. "So, you fellas going back all the way to Denver tonight? You're welcome to bunk down with us. Lots of room downstairs."

"Thanks, but we'll drive back tonight," replied John, shifting in his saddle to ease the pain in his backside.

Keith spoke for everyone. "Jack, I just wanna thank you for this weekend. I can't remember enjoying any outing half this much before."

Tom and John followed with words of gratitude. Donny even gave an appreciative grunt, though his pain far outweighed any pleasure he'd had.

"Well, I'd be happy to have you all back another time," said Jack. Thanks from these men were more important than all the money they could pay him.

"Whadya say, fellas?" asked Tom. "Make this an annual event? The four of us back here hunting bear again next May?"

"OK by me," said Keith.

John glanced appreciatively at the bearskin slung across a packhorse. "I'm coming back, with or without you tenderfoots. I got hooked last spring, and I'll write this trip into my calendar every year."

Donny rode along in painful silence.

"Come on, Donny. Let's you and me bury the hatchet," said Tom, riding up even and extending his right hand. "I'm sorry for bad-mouthing you this morning. You know I don't mean nothing by it."

Donny slowly offered Tom a limp-wristed handshake. "Forget it. It's over and done."

Tom whacked Donny's shoulder. "Ain't over till I buy you the biggest steak in all of Colorado tonight. OK?"

"OK."

"You're gonna come back with us next year, aren't you, Donny?" asked Keith.

Donny chuckled. "No, boys, I liked this weekend real fine, but it's kind of like when we took that trip to the Grand Canyon a few years back. Once you seen it, ain't no need to go back again."

"Sounds like it's just the three of us next year, boys," said Tom. "The Three Musketeers."

Jack laughed and said, "More like the three musty steers."

♦   ♦   ♦

As he watched the hunting party pass through the gate and start up the driveway, Sergeant Julius Straub, lying in wait on his belly in the stable loft, sighted down the barrel of the .30-30. He had stationed a man on the second-floor ranch-house balcony, another just inside the front entry downstairs, and the fourth man out behind the pig barn. Their mandate was simple—kill everything that moves.

♦   ♦   ♦

As Jack and the party approached, he looked around to see that all was well. The house, the barn, the corrals, and stable outside the picket fence by some twenty yards; the sun, now a big orange ball on the mountain slope, had all but left the valley; there were only a handful of horses in the stable, but nothing was unusual about that. Joe often cut them loose to graze in the pasture. It struck him as a little strange that Sarge hadn't come out to greet them, but he was probably in the house asleep.

At the corral, the men dismounted and gathered their belongings from the packhorses.

"Wade'll take care of the horses," Jack said. "That *is* why God created young people, isn't it, preacher?"

The men handed over their reins, and Wade led the horses into the corral.

"Son, when you're finished, bring that bear skin on up to the house."

"Will do, Pa."

"You can shower up a'fore you go, guys."

"Now that we won't turn down," Keith said, and he slapped Jack appreciatively on the back.

"And I'll have Hilda rustle some grub while you're cleanin' up."

"Thanks, Jack, but we got our sights set on that mining camp restaurant in Cokedale," John said. "Looks like a neat place to eat."

"It's a good place," Jack said. "All the beans and homemade bread you can swallow, and thick steaks fixed whatever way you like 'um."

Laden with backpacks, blankets, and rifles, Jack and the four, Donny, Keith, John, and Tom started toward the house together. They were passing through the gate in the picket fence, when Jack said, "Whoa! You men stop and make sure those guns are unloaded before you take 'um in." He broke open the action of his double-barreled backup gun and was about to pull the shells from the chambers when he said to John, "You know, I just remembered those bear teeth of yours in my saddle bag. I'll go back and get 'um." As he turned, he stopped again, this time, suddenly.

"What...?" he said.

Not twenty yards away, a big man was leaning out of the stable loft, and he had a rifle in his hands—aimed at Jack.

Jack Carson had never had been shot at in his life, but instinct sent him sprawling just a fraction of a second before the report of a rifle boomed across the yard. He felt a sting in his neck, but as he heard the double clack-clack sound of a cartridge being levered into a chamber, he slammed the action of his backup gun shut, swung it up, and instinctively fired. The heavy pellets struck the man in the shoulder and slammed him back inside the loft.

The four astounded hunters, standing like deer caught in the headlamp of a speeding locomotive, were too shocked to move.

As murderous gunfire poured out from what seemed like everywhere, Jack rolled to the cover of a pine tree and looked up to see—hardly a dozen feet from where he now lay—John, Keith, Tom, and Donny all shot up and dropping to the ground. John died instantly, his back ripped open by merciless 7-mm fire. Keith was struck twice and died seconds later, his face half shot away and a whole the size of a baseball in his upper abdomen. Tom was gut shot by the man on the balcony and left bleeding like a butchered pig. He'd lay squirming in pitiful childish sobs before passing on. Donny lay writhing in the dust squealing in a voice shrill with horror from a bullet wound to his shoulder.

Jack peered about. From somewhere he heard whimpering and groaning. Where was Wade? Then he saw him, the boy's eyes wide, peering around the corner of the stable. Another gunshot, and fragments of wood flew from the stable door, and Jack saw Wade duck for cover.

Suddenly, a man ran from the pig barn toward the stable, and a blast from Jack's scattergun kicked his feet out from under him and landed him hard on the ground.

Jack threw open the breech of his double, slipped in two more shells, and lay still while the fusillade began again. Seething in torment at the sight of his four friends lying in tangled heaps on the hard ground, he asked why. *Why?* What was this *about!*

A sudden stab of fear tore at his gut as he pictured Cassie and Josh and the Koivunens. But he would have to wait to learn more about their well-being. He glanced over his shoulder to see his son again peering around the corner of the stable. "Wade! stay down!" he yelled. "You hear me? Stay *down!*"

But Wade was gazing on the unimaginable devastation before him, his thoughts flying in all directions, his heart hammering with fear. He answered back in a quivering voice, "I'll stay down, Pa, but I gotta do *somethin'*! Where's Josh and Cassie?" Then he heard his father shouting.

"There's one above you there in the loft, Wade! He's hit hard, but keep a watch out for him."

Wade looked up at the planks above him and saw dust sifting down. Then glancing out through the door, he saw a man dart from the house and vault the picket fence. "Pa, one of 'um's just made a break for the carriage house…"

"I seen him, son. Now you just stay where you are!"

But Wade couldn't stay still. Desperate, he leaped up and ran to his horse, still saddled and tethered, and snatched from the saddle scabbard, the .45-70 lever action saddle gun he'd carried for the bear hunt. With it, he rolled under the corral fence and ran around back of the stable—his father still calling to him to stay down—then slowing, he stealthily crouched toward the old carriage house. With his pa pinned down by the man on the balcony, this one was probably trying to flank him.

With the carriage house in view, Wade settled in to wait. It was then he heard a thin wail in the air, and with it, sobbing. "Cassie? Josh?" he asked himself.

Meanwhile, Jack, pinned on his belly and knowing there was a man in the carriage house, was holding down the one on the balcony with pistol fire.

Then, unexpectedly, the man in the carriage house appeared, and from somewhere came a fierce explosion that blew the man clear out of Jack's sight. Jack lay there—wondering. And then he called, "Wade?"

"Yes, Pa!"

"Wade—did you do that?"

"Yes, Pa…me and my .45-70!"

Jack muttered to himself, "My Lord! *That* fella's gone for good."

Now with the odds narrowed, Jack thought, that one on the balcony was as good as dead. He slipped two more buckshot-loaded shells into his backup gun, got to his feet, stepped out from behind the tree, and let go. The balcony railing that had hidden the sniper flew into the air and came bouncing and clattering down and off the roof.

Before the man behind it could reload, Jack's second discharge sent him careening off the balcony onto the ground, where he lay unmoving. Jack watched for a moment to be sure, reloading as he watched. Then a sudden burst of sound from the stable made him look around.

There, the big man with his mangled shoulder and dangling arm burst out astride his horse and fled like a fox with its tail on fire. Jack slammed the action of his double closed, and emptied both barrels. But by now the distance was too great for even the buckshot to reach him.

With their attackers gone and the shooting stilled, Wade emerged from behind the stable and joined his dad just outside the picket fence. Then rose a bloodcurdling howl, and they saw Donny's huge body writhing on the ground.

They ignored Donny and raced to the house, dreading what they would find.

They found nothing; no one was there.

Jack's heart thumped like a trip hammer, and his head ached. While Wade continued to search, Jack rushed out the back door, hurdling the remains of his prized twelve-year-old German shepherd Sarge as though he hadn't seen it, his only thoughts now of Josh and Cassie, and Joe and Hilda.

Back in the front yard, he heard a voice and looked down.

"*Bitte, schiesse. Bitte.*"

"What…" Jack stared at the wounded young man before him, his lower body blood-drenched, his left hand holding in his exposed intestines, and two bones of his right arm protruding from the skin, broken when he fell from the balcony. "*Bitte?*" Jack said.

"*Bitte enschiesse mich,*" repeated the man, his tearful eyes and raw voice were pleading…but pleading for what?

Jack, in slow, astonished tones, said, "You're *German*," and suddenly he knew what this was about—the German POW camp at Trinidad. These men were escaped prisoners. He bent over the young man. "My *children*," Jack said. "Where are my *children*?"

The POW returned a puzzled look, gripping Jack's arm with his left hand, and gasping for breath; he was suffocating.

Then from behind Jack came a familiar voice. "*Die kinder*." Jack turned and looked up to see Wade, who had learned a little German from the Koivunens. "*Wo bist die kinder*?" Wade said.

His dark face clouded, the young man turned his pain-ridden eyes in the direction of Raton Pass and pointed his one good arm that way. "*Mit mein colonel*," he muttered.

"With my colonel," Wade said.

"Raton Pass?" asked Jack.

The dying soldier nodded.

Jack felt a surge of elation and an easing in his chest; perhaps his children were still alive. "And the Koivunens?" He turned to Wade. "Ask him about Joe and Hilda."

"*Bitte, schiesse. Bitte.*" The man said again.

Wade looked at his dad. "Pa, he's beggin' you to kill him. He's hurtin' too bad."

"Oh, God!" Jack muttered and looked down at the man—who really was no more than a boy. No older than Wade—Wade who himself would soon be in this war.

Jack gazed on him, wondering what he himself would want a stranger to do if this were Wade. As he gazed, the young man suddenly convulsed; a little river of deep red blood swelled up in his mouth and spilled out and down the side of his face to the ground. The red, unseeing eyes, now fixed on the darkening sky, glazed over with death.

Jack let out a deep breath. "We'll learn no more from him," he whispered. "Mercifully, he's gone." He paused, then said, "…Merciful to him, and merciful to me."

He closed the boy's eyes and rose from his knees. "Let's check on the others," he said.

Donny's companions were dead, and Donny, wild with agony, lay writhing on the blood-soaked grass.

"Get the truck," commanded Jack, wiping a blood trickle from his own neck. "We'll load Donny on it and get him to the hospital in Segundo."

Wade sprinted to the truck as Jack leaned over to comfort the hunting four-some's sole survivor.

Tears filled Donny's big brown eyes. "Don't let me die!" he wailed.

"We ain't gonna let you die, Donny. We're taking you on into Segundo to get fixed up. You gotta stay calm now, you hear? Don't let yourself go into shock."

"Who done this…who done this to us, Jack?"

"Some escaped German prisoners. I'm going after 'um now. You got my word—we'll make 'um pay for what they done here."

Donny gawked about, wild-eyed. "The others?"

"There's nothing we can do for 'um, Donny. Now you just relax and save your strength. We'll have you in Segundo in no time."

As they struggled to load Donny's great body onto the flatbed truck, Jack said to Wade, "You take him straight to Segundo. Our phone and radio have been shot to pieces. Have the authorities there get in touch with the army at Trinidad. Tell 'um some of their prisoners got Josh and Cassie and the Koivunens and made off on horseback for Raton Pass. You hear?"

"Yeah, Pa. You going after 'um?"

"Yes, I am, son."

"Pa, you gotta wait up for me and let me go along."

Jack raised a hand to ward him off. "No time. I gotta leave now, and I need you to see Donny to the hospital. Hear? Just tell the army the POWs are making a break through Raton Pass on into New Mexico, likely headed for the Mexican border. I'll stay in touch, son."

"OK, Pa. I'll tell 'um, but you be careful."

Jack reached to smother Wade in his arms—the first time he'd done that in years. "I'm very proud of you, son. You saved my life here today."

Wade welcomed his father's embrace. "I'm proud of you too, Pa."

"Good. Now get on to Segundo afore Donny bleeds to death."

As Wade leapt into the truck and sped out of the yard, he marveled at the irony. Here he was—all signed up to go overseas to fight the war, and darned if the war hadn't come right to his own front door.

◆   ◆   ◆

Jack was desperate to set out in search of his children, but something told him the Koivunens had never left the yard. Full of dread, he headed for the stables.

When he reached the door and peered inside, he saw them; the remains of Joe and Hilda, the sickly seal of death having long settled upon their sweet innocent faces. Wracked with grief, Jack dropped to his knees, convulsed, and unleashed mighty tears of sorrow for the first time since his beloved Melissa died four years ago.

But a minute later, he was riding off in headlong pursuit of the men who had stolen away his beloved Josh and Cassie, willing to lay down his very life to see them free.

10

The late sun was now nearly lost to the mountain slopes, but to Jack Carson, that was only an annoyance.

With tears running down his face, his lips moved in prayer for the well-being of his children. An empty ache gnawed at him as anxiety and determination pushed him on toward Raton Pass. The mountains around the pass were now black profiles against a darkening sky.

The big, wounded POW who'd ridden out would be dead soon. Nothing touched by that scattergun had ever lived to tell about it. But the man was no concern to Jack—except for the blood trail he had left behind. As long as there was enough light for him to see the black smudges and puddles that streaked the dead needles and leaves, he could follow. From the amount of blood, he supposed this man had an hour, maybe two—if he was strong and very lucky.

It was well past suppertime now, but Jack didn't think of food or of rest or sleep. This was a flat-out race to overtake his precious children and the godless trash who'd abducted them. With his blood on the boil, his jaw set, and his senses razor sharp, he rode into a near-impenetrable growth of blue spruce, ponderosa, and aspen on the shoulders of Mount Baldy.

Jack's horse, Comanche, old and ugly as sin—but his most reliable—labored under Jack's weight to mount the sharp incline. Jack was worried about Comanche—he'd known little rest this day and now Jack was pushing him to his limits.

Jack's mouth was gritty and dry, and his face tinged with dirt and sweat. Without slowing, he clenched his canteen and took a long swallow of warm water. What agony! Even Melissa's death hadn't hurt like this. The image of the beloved Koivunens lying dead in the straw burned in his brain, and Josh and Cassie were in the grasp of the man who'd murdered them. Once they'd outlived their usefulness, he would kill them too. He must overtake them this side of the pass…and night was coming on, the sky growing dark.

A single rifle shot pierced the peaceable mountain air. Jack pulled up and listened hard. What could it be? Josh? Cassie? He dismounted and took to his feet to rest Comanche. This was rocky, heavily wooded country with deep, dark gorges. The climb was steep and getting steeper, but Jack had no quit in him. He had to get to Raton Pass before the POWs got there, or lose them to the vast New Mexican wilderness.

It was an hour later when once more rifle fire shattered the stillness—again, a single gunshot.

"What in *tarnation*!" exclaimed Jack as though old Comanche could understand. Suddenly the light came on. The rifle shots were a beacon to draw the bushwhackers to the main body. This was the break he needed.

Driven by a raging impatience, he mounted Comanche and spurred him on in the direction of the rifle fire. If he could find them under cover of darkness, he'd have a fighting chance.

◆   ◆   ◆

Sergeant Straub heard the second shot. Half unconscious from loss of blood and desperately confused, he halted his mount and strained to hear—or perhaps to see a flicker of firelight among the trees. The sound of the gunshot had echoed so—first from this mountainside and then from that—and the trees had damped the sound. Which direction had it come from? But he pressed his mount on, taking his chances, eager to rest and to get the medical help he so desperately needed.

◆   ◆   ◆

In the darkness, the POWs sat around a blazing fire, drinking coffee and eating the sandwiches Hilda and Cassie had fixed for them. The campfire lit the black-silhouetted treetops that stood moving just a little in the cool evening breeze. The yelp of a timber wolf deep in the forest, the rhythmical thud of distant ax blows, and the crackling of the roaring fire were all that disturbed the mountain peace.

Josh lay on a blanket not far from the fire, his hands and feet bound. He imagined his father and brother long dead, but he prayed for them anyway, prayed until his soul hurt.

Cassie, who had fallen into a hard silence, sat peering off into the gloomy darkness, devoid of hope. Bound like her brother and leaning her head against a tree, she felt that nothing short of suicide could take away her suffering. Now she saw the young dark-haired, blue-eyed German named Georg coming toward her with a plate of food in his hands.

"You must eat, young lady," he said in a kind, quiet voice.

"I'm not hungry," Cassie said. She stared at the sandwiches and thought of Hilda, how her hands had touched them, how she would never see Hilda again.

"The colonel has ordered me to watch over you," Georg said. "And I'm glad. I *want* to help you. Please eat."

But Cassie closed her mouth tight and looked away.

"We'll not likely take time for breakfast in the morning," said Georg. "Please, eat the sandwich."

"I won't eat with murderers," Cassie said in a tone close to madness. She wrinkled her nose and filled her pale blue eyes with cold contempt. "I hope you choke on yours."

"We are not all murderers," Georg argued, speaking from his heart. "I wanted nothing to do with this. It was all Colonel Von Toth's doing. The rest of us were dragged along with no say in the matter."

From the blanket where he lay, Josh broke in. "You'll hang sure as the sunrise when they catch up with you—and they *will* catch up with you."

Georg looked at the boy, not all that much younger than himself. The boy's steely, ice-cold gaze was full of hate.

"You're every bit as responsible as your commander for what happened today."

Georg bit his lip. "Yes," he said. "If they catch us, I will hang. Even so, we were only following orders as good soldiers must. I…" He had started to say that he would go to his grave with a clear conscience, but perhaps he would not. Perhaps the faces of the old people Von Toth had killed before his eyes today would haunt him forever. It wasn't hanging he dreaded so, but that these two might be right. Maybe he was as much to blame as Von Toth.

"And you'll rot in hell to boot," said a grim-faced Cassie.

"Well…" Georg said. "Enough of this; you must eat."

Again, Cassie turned her face away, and Georg turned to Josh and looked him in the eyes. "So, Josh, will you be so foolish as your sister?"

Josh looked at the sandwiches, and he, too, thought of Hilda. But, he also thought of what had to be done. Soon push could well come to shove, and he'd need every ounce of strength he could muster. He must eat. "No," his subdued voice still had an edge. "I'll eat," and then he began to struggle to sit up. "Cut me loose," he said.

"No. I can't do that," Georg said. "Here, let me help you." He reached down, took Josh by the shoulder, and when he had raised him up, steadied him with his hand and began to feed him.

After eating, Josh again lay down, and in brooding silence, gazed up beyond the treetops. With a moon only three nights old now hanging over the white-capped Sangre De Cristos, the sky was dark, and the stars had come out. Never had he seen the stars so cold. Fighting to quell the rage in his brain, tears running down the sides of his head into his hair, he felt something deep within his spirit growing hard.

Georg decided it was best not to engage either Cassie or Josh again, so he called for a comrade to keep watch as he stepped away to warm himself at the fire. He was still thinking about what they had said to him. What *should* he have done? What *could* he have done to save them? Boe and Radmanovich and the two old people? Would his own death have changed anything? Was it better to be killed than to kill? He couldn't decide.

He, too, gazed up at the tops of the pine trees, their silhouettes sharp and blacker even than the black sky. The tops of the trees were swaying a little in the quickening, cold night wind. The firmament directly above was clear and busy with stars. Cold stars, he thought, after this day's work. From amid the peaks to the west, lightning flashed, and distant thunder gave notice of a coming storm.

He was lost in these thoughts when a sound in the brush made him and his comrades turn their heads, weapons at the ready.

"Who goes there?" asked Von Toth in his native German tongue.

"Colonel" a voice came back, "…it's me…Straub."

Straub was still astride his horse, but barely.

When Von Toth saw him, he stiffened. Straub's bloody left arm hung limp from a mangled shoulder. His face was pasty and swollen, his lower lip turned inside out, his eyes barely visible, and he seemed about to fall from the horse's back.

Von Toth made no move to go to him, but he demanded, "The other men, Straub?"

"Dead, my colonel," Straub answered as two fellow soldiers gently eased him from his saddle and laid him by the fire.

In the darkness away from the fire, Josh and Cassie could make nothing of these German words, but seeing the big man, they knew things had not gone as planned. Suddenly they were breathing the light breath of hope, their hearts alive again with promise.

"And Jack Carson, Straub? You did away with this man?" inquired the colonel, his dark brows knitted with unrest.

Cassie recognized her father's name and let out a little cry of hope.

Straub's vague, pain-drenched eyes rolled back of his eye lids as he answered. "No, my colonel. He's alive...he and a young man."

"Georg," whispered Josh.

Georg came near, a furtive smile on his face, and whispered, "It is good news. Your father and a young man survived the shooting."

"Yes!" Josh exclaimed. Again, with Georg's help, he struggled to a sitting position, gave his sister a wide, tearful smile, and felt the thing that had grown hard in his spirit growing soft again.

Even as her eyes filled with tears, Cassie's heart thumped with delight.

Now they watched Colonel Von Toth as he stepped away from where the sergeant lay. The unease in his face of a few moments ago had recast itself into full-fledged fear.

"I am sorry, my colonel," uttered Straub. Deep pain filled his vacant eyes, and tears of torment spilled down his cheeks.

Von Toth turned away from him and said into the darkness, "Twice you have disappointed me this day, Sergeant...and now you've left a blood trail to bring this mountain man down on us."

Georg knelt and spread a blanket over Straub and set to cleaning and dressing his wounds. "He's lost much blood, Herr Colonel. But with care..."

At this, Von Toth turned back to look into the face of this man who had once served him so well but now had failed him so bitterly. Surely, he thought, Straub has been my true friend. He sighed and shook his head with regret, then looked at Georg. "But rest and proper care are luxuries we cannot afford. The sergeant would only slow us down."

Georg could hardly believe it. He stood and confronted Von Toth to his face. "Herr Colonel, if it pleases you, sir, any one of these men could remain here with Sergeant Straub and care for him until he is able to ride while we go on...or *I* myself will stay behind. Our chances of reaching Mexico on our own might not be good, but trying would be better than..." Georg did not want to speak the words out loud. As he stood watching Von Toth's eyes, he thought perhaps there was a chance, and then...

"I think not," Von Toth said, and drew his pistol.

"No, Colonel!" Georg said. "Surely you will not...!"

"Georg! I will this moment hang you from that limb if you oppose me!" And with that he knelt beside Straub and in an almost tender voice, spoke to him as one would speak to a small child. "You were a good soldier once, Straub. A very *fine* soldier. But, my old friend, for you, the fight is over."

From under his blankets and bandages, with bruised face and swollen eyes, Sergeant Julius Straub gazed up at his colonel. His stomach contracted into a tight ball, and he looked with disbelief at the drawn pistol. Yet he spoke not a word. As he resigned himself to his death, he closed his eyes, and tears were running down the sides of his head.

The colonel drew the blanket over Straub's face, put the pistol to his temple, and squeezed the trigger. The .45 automatic bucked in Von Toth's hand and its voice spread among the trees and echoed off the surrounding mountains.

Cassie and Josh and Georg looked on, astonished and sick. Georg thought he saw a quiver in the colonel's chin, and wondered if he was blinking back tears.

Von Toth stood to his feet and gazed down on them all. "What are you all staring at?" he said. "I could do no other than what I've done! You think I've no heart? Well, you're right. I lost what heart I had to an American P-47 in the deserts of North Africa. All I have to live for now is defending our glorious Fatherland. Have you anything in your miserable lives so glorious to live for as that?" He waited for an answer, then said, "I doubt that you do."

11

The sky was clear and dark. The sliver of moon visible only an hour ago, was now veiled by the approaching clouds and provided no light. The distant thunder Georg had heard was closer now, the sound coming to them on a cold wind that rushed down the mountain from the northwest, sighing in the trees and threatening rain or snow.

Sure now that Jack Carson was somewhere out in the night, Colonel Von Toth had ordered the crackling fire in the pit extinguished. There was nothing but the sound of the wind among the pines and a solitary shovel preparing Sergeant Straub's final resting place.

Georg had just checked the ropes on Josh and Cassie's wrists and feet when he heard Von Toth's voice speaking to him in German. He looked up at his superior's beckoning.

"Georg, may I have a word with you?"

Georg left his securely bound charges resting beneath warm blankets and hurried over.

The colonel was holding a cup of hot coffee, and a cigarette lay nestled in the corner of his mouth. He looked up and exhaled a cloud of smoke in Georg's direction. "I want the children gagged from here on." He picked up something from beneath his right thigh. "Here," he said, "I tore these strips of flannel from one of the shirts we took from the Carson place. Take them and gag the children; we can't have them crying out when their father is near."

"Yes, my colonel. The boy Josh wants me to tell you that we cannot push the horses as hard tomorrow. They'll not last us long in this rugged country if we do."

"Yes, but we now have Straub's mount, and we'll have two more once the children have seen us through Raton Pass tomorrow afternoon."

"Two more, sir?"

"Yes. The children won't be any good to us in New Mexico. We'll eliminate them and make good use of their horses. That will make nearly two horses for every man. We'll be able to rest half of them at a time."

"Eliminate the children, Colonel? Couldn't we simply release them on foot…so far now from civilization?"

Von Toth flicked his cigarette to the ground, sipped his coffee, and spoke with brutal indifference. "I've considered releasing them, but their deaths will serve a much greater purpose. You see, Carson will hear the shots and come running. He'll find their bodies in a clearing. Delirious with heartache, he'll rush to their sides, directly into my waiting gun sites. No more worrying about the legendary Jack Carson hunting us down."

Georg's mouth hung open. He was astonished. Never had he knowingly been in the presence of cold, irrational evil. And now he was. This man's eyes and mind were like a dark well that had no bottom. He blinked and shifted nervously, and then, rags in hand, he got to his feet. "Yes, sir," he said. "I'll see to it that the children are gagged."

Von Toth stood and gave him a wintry stare. "You haven't much stomach for this kind of thing, have you?"

"No, sir," Georg said, "I do not."

"Well, just see that you obey my orders without question. You second-guess one of my decisions again, and you'll live to regret it."

"Yes, sir."

Von Toth's expression softened, and Georg drew back his head just a little and felt his lip curl as the colonel reached up, patted him softly on the cheek, and resting his hand there, spoke in almost fatherly tones.

"You know, Georg, the Americans have a saying, 'Nice guys finish last.' You and I will rejoin our comrades in defense of our glorious Fatherland *only* if we set aside all pretense of moral conduct and persevere without question. Germany has many enemies, but she will prevail because her people boast one quality the others lack—a sense of duty and unquestioned loyalty." He jerked his head toward the children. "People like these Carsons—given the chance—will destroy you. They've already killed four of our number, and they'll kill again if we let them." He slowly removed his hand from Georg's cheek. "Now go do what I told you."

As Georg turned away, he found himself trembling with the strangest sensation. It was though a hooded cobra had swayed before him and he had looked it in the eyes and not been bitten.

Or had he?

At that moment, one of Von Toth's men emerged from the brush, pointing back and whispering, "Colonel Von Toth, someone's coming!"

Von Toth turned back to Georg. "Gag them!"

Georg hurried back and, waking them, put the cloths between their teeth and knotted them tightly behind their heads. In answer to their frightened stares, he put his finger to his lips, thinking that Von Toth had just planted a seedling of treason in his soul.

When he turned back toward Von Toth, he saw him and two others kneeling, awaiting Jack Carson's approach. He listened. Yes—the unmistakable clump of hooves was coming straight for them.

The colonel raised the stolen .30-30 rifle, and a celebratory gleam lighted his face.

At that moment, the dark figure of a man mounted and with a packhorse in tow, obviously oblivious to his danger, came into view from among the trees.

Von Toth took up the slack in the trigger, eager now to end this man's life.

"Hey, anybody home?" It was the voice of an old man.

Von Toth lowered his rifle, provoked to find that the hunched and grizzled old man before them was not the renowned Jack Carson. "Yes, yes, come on in," he answered.

The old man strained his eyes to see the men rising up out of the brush. "Seen yer fire from a ways back, and thought I'd come see who'd be fool crazy enough to be out in this neck of the woods this time of year."

"Bear hunters," replied Von Toth. "Very *frustrated* bear hunters. And you, sir?"

The old man dismounted, stretched his shriveled, rickety-looking old body, and gave vent to an enormous yawn.

"Well, first off, I ain't no '*sir*.'" He extended his right hand to Von Toth, grinning through a ratty gray beard. "And, second, the name's Anderson, *Trapper* Anderson."

Von Toth accepted the handshake. "Bill Thomas. You're alone this evening?"

"Yeah, I'm alone. Alone *every* evenin'. That is, if yer talkin' about people. Got me a whole woods full of God's finest critters to keep me comp'ny. Bear hunters, eh?" Anderson's grin revealed stained and crooked teeth. He rubbed his whiskers with the knuckles of his right hand and asked in a whiskey voice, "Jack Carson guidin' ya?"

"No, we have no guide," said Von Toth with a forced smile and a shake of his head. "We're alone out here."

"Well, no *wonder* yer frustrated! Next time out, give old Jack a dingle. He'll fix ya up with a bear, sure as shootin'. City fellers, ain't ya?"

Seeing little point in furthering this conversation, the colonel unobtrusively slipped the hunting knife from its leather scabbard about his waist. "Yes, city fellers. You haven't by chance come upon this Jack Carson today, have you?"

"No, sirree. Ain't seen hide nor hair of old Jack the better part of a month now."

Back in the shadows, Josh and Cassie recognized the old recluse. Trapping, hunting, fishing—he did whatever it took to keep him alive in the mountains that he'd been born in and always said he'd never step foot out of. Reclusive but friendly, he'd do anything you asked of him. Shaggy gray hair, uncut and unwashed, spilled ingloriously from a dirty old hat, and he wore a bear tooth necklace slung around his neck. His body screamed of neglect; he had rotted, yellow teeth, an unruly beard, and a face scarred beyond repair from a fight with a fatally wounded black bear. He'd been to the ranch many a time for coffee and occasionally stayed for a meal. Josh and Cassie had, on occasion, ridden up to his old log cabin a few miles above the ranch. They'd never forget the canned pears and peaches he'd favor them with. Now terrified as they watched, their eyes brimmed with tears.

Without hesitation, Von Toth swung his left arm around the old man's throat and thrust the blade into his back.

His eyes wild, his face a mask of terror, Anderson let out a muffled groan as he slowly collapsed at the colonel's feet.

◆   ◆   ◆

As Wade Carson paced the barracks at Camp Trinidad, there was no hiding his frustration that the army insisted on waiting until daybreak to set out after the POWs. There was no chance now to catch up before the fugitives squeezed through the natural bottleneck known as Raton Pass.

When the POW work party had failed to turn up at the mines, the army had dispatched every available man to hunt them down and needed time now to regroup. The good news was that army and civilian units from far and wide planned a massive manhunt in the New Mexican wilderness at first light.

12

Scant sunlight broke through a clouded eastern horizon as Colonel Von Toth was relieving himself a few yards into the brush. He realized that Jack Carson would have alerted the authorities to their whereabouts, and that their odds against escaping were now much greater. Every gun-toting lawman and vigilante in New Mexico would be on their trail.

Meanwhile, Georg Dreschler was up seeing to his charges. He had wakened them, gently removed the rags from their mouths, and fed them beef jerky and warm water.

"We've a long way to go, and you must have strength," he told them.

This time, Cassie didn't turn the food away.

Georg had not slept well; his mind had been busy concocting escape. So tight was Von Toth's circle of guards that he'd not dared cut Josh and Cassie loose in the night. Now, with the colonel out in the woods, he could talk with them.

As he bent over Cassie to feed her, he whispered. "Listen, once you've seen us through the pass, my colonel plans to kill you."

At this Josh and Cassie tensed and looked at each other in alarm.

"Yes," Georg said. "It's terrifying. But I will help you. When I see an opening I'll cut you free and we'll make our break. You watch for my sign. Josh, once you're free, you must lead the way. Understood?"

Josh and Cassie nodded and gave each other and Georg mystified looks.

"Thank you," said Cassie with a weak smile.

"Don't thank me until we've escaped this madman." He fed her the last piece of jerky and smiled at her. "All right. Now I must gag you again."

As Georg retied her gag, Cassie felt something very strange. For the first time, she noticed how gently Georg was working, how cautious he was not to hurt her, and how he seemed to purposely brush her neck with his hands and her lips with his fingers, how when he was done, he placed his hands on her shoulders and looked reassuringly into her eyes. And she noticed for the first time how wonderfully his pale blue eyes contrasted with his coal black hair. It stunned her a little. How odd, she thought, when only hours ago, she *hated* him!

And then, back among the trees, when the colonel had finished and was starting back to camp, he heard the unmistakable sound of a pistol being cocked at his right ear. It chilled him to the very bone.

"One sound, Colonel, and I'll blow your head clean off."

Von Toth took a deep breath and cleared his throat. In a labored, barely restrained tone, he responded, "Jack Carson. I am deeply honored, sir, to make your acquaintance."

Jack pressed the pistol barrel into the colonel's ear. His voice was full of wrath, every muscle taut. "You listen up, Colonel, and you listen up good. You got three men standing guard out there. Call 'um in now. We're gonna have us a little powwow in the clearing."

Von Toth called out in German. "Sentries, come back in. We're moving out. Everyone prepare to ride."

"I hope for your sake that was word for word. Now…you and me are gonna walk on in," growled Jack. "One wrong move and I'll end your pitiful existence. You hear?"

"I find myself at a distinct disadvantage, Jack Carson. Be assured, you have my full cooperation. No doubt you have some method to your madness here that you'll kindly share with me. After all, I do have eight armed and highly skilled men for you to deal with. Eight-to-one odds are a bit much, even for a man of your considerable stature."

"I assure you, Colonel, I'd already have laid waste to you and your highly skilled little buddies if it weren't for my kids being caught in the middle of all this. Now, next thing that's gonna come out of your mouth is you tellin' your boys to stand down and not do anything heroic. That is, if you value your life."

"I haven't heard your plan."

"Just keep movin' and do as I say. Tell your boys to leave their weapons in place. You'll hear my plan soon enough."

The three lookouts ambled into the clearing just ahead of Jack and the colonel.

With his arms raised high, Von Toth said in German, "Now hear me. Do as the mountain man says. No gunplay."

Josh and Cassie first gaped in wonder, then squealed and laughed through their gags.

Jack glanced toward them, his heart on the verge of breaking at the sight of them trussed up like pigs. He addressed Georg, who stood next to the youngsters.

"Cut 'um free and take those gags off." Then to Von Toth. "Colonel, you tell these boys there's been a change in plans. I assume you brought my children along to guide you through Raton Pass. My young'uns are gonna ride out safe while I stay behind to be your guide."

Von Toth silently turned his head to look at Jack's face, wondering if he had heard correctly. For a moment, they stared into each other's eyes. Von Toth felt a slow smile spreading on his lips, and then he turned his face toward his men and translated word for word.

When Georg cut the ropes on their hands, the children pulled off their own gags, leaped up, and ran to their father's side with tears streaming down their faces.

Keeping focused on Von Toth, Jack wrapped his left arm around his beloved daughter and kissed her hair. He said, "Your brother's doing just fine back at the ranch, kids." And then, discreetly, he shoved a note into the pocket of her jeans and shot her a wink, saying, "You and Josh mount up and get outta here. Now!"

She nodded her understanding and released her grip on his arm.

But Josh didn't move. "Pa, you're *crazy* to stay behind here with this rotten son of Satan!" exclaimed Josh. His breath quickened in desperation. "He'll *kill* you, sure as hellfire. You can ride out with us now. Ain't none of these cowards gonna try to stop us—not with you holding that handgun on 'um."

"Your father's much too smart for that," mocked Von Toth, "and he cares too much for the two of you to hazard your lives in a gunfight."

"Pa, we could take the colonel hostage," wailed Cassie, tears blurring her eyes. "The others wouldn't shoot at us with him along."

With a stone-like face, Von Toth said, "My dear, do you really think I would be stupid enough to ride out of here with you to face a hanging? Your father knows I'd never agree to that. What assurance can you give me, Carson, that once I've allowed your children to ride off, you won't simply shoot me in the back and run off through the trees?"

"You have my word on it. That's all you get. You give my kids a chance to ride clear of here and I give you my word to turn this pistol over to you."

"Fair enough," replied Von Toth.

Jack was pained to see the terror in his children's eyes. But there simply was no better way out. "Listen, both of you," he said. "I want you on your horses and heading back to the ranch. No more talk, kids. One of these here boys is likely to get a little trigger happy if we keep talking much longer."

"But, Pa!" bawled Cassie.

"*Go*, Cassie! Can't you understand? We got no more cards to play here. Josh, see your sister to those horses and ride out now. You hear?"

Josh started to argue, but knew it would do no good. Tears clouded his vision as he said, "Bye, Pa. We're gonna see you again!"

Jack smiled through his pain. "Soon, Josh," he said, "Real soon." He drew the sobbing Cassie near and kissed her forehead. "Go on now, honey. Please do as I say."

Cassie's gaze fell upon Georg, the one face in this crowd of men that gave her hope. Yes. Georg—he'd see to her pa's escape the same as he would have seen to theirs. She hugged her father one more time and looked at Georg, her eyes pleading with him.

Josh, too, glanced at Georg and left his father's side with a glimmer of hope. Brother and sister mounted up and took one last look at their beloved father. Never had they loved him as they did at this moment.

13

When Josh and Cassie had been gone a good ten minutes, Jack tossed his weapon to the ground and backed away from Colonel Von Toth. He'd given his word to this shameful wretch, and Jack Carson was the kind of man whose word meant more to him than life itself. Besides, he'd not likely survive a shootout with this many professional soldiers. He now felt the noose around his neck. Even so, he stood with shoulders squared and head held high.

Jack watched the colonel's face flush with rage and satisfaction and looked into his hard, angry eyes.

Von Toth drew the .45 army automatic he had taken from Boe, and pressed its muzzle against Jack's nose. "Get down on your knees," he said, his tone heavy with contempt.

Jack knelt.

"I promise you, mountain man, you'll live to regret my sparing your worthless life. You'd have done better to turn that gun on yourself than to throw yourself at my mercy."

Jack looked up into Von Toth's eyes. "Mercy, Colonel? Does a man of your sort know the meaning of that word?"

Von Toth swung the pistol at Jack's nose, smashing it and sending blood spewing. "I see now where your children get their insolence, Mr. Carson."

Von Toth turned and addressed Georg in a low voice. "Bind his hands. The rest of you saddle up. We leave in ten minutes."

Hiding his relief that Von Toth had not killed Jack outright, Georg brought rope, and as he wound and tightened and knotted it about Jack's wrists, he tried to give him small signals of his friendship—a fleeting connection of his eyes with Jack's, a sympathetic touch to his hand, a grip of his arm so quick and hidden that no one but Jack knew. Did it work? Did Jack understand? A quizzical look from Jack's eyes showed him that he did.

Georg stepped aside and watched as Jack and Von Toth faced each other down.

Jack, standing defiantly while the blood ran down and dripped from his chin, smirked through his pain as he growled, "You ain't got a snowball's chance in hell of getting outta here, Colonel. We sent word to the army that you was heading for Raton Pass. They're gonna hunt you down like riders and hounds after a fox."

"And you would suggest," Von Toth said sarcastically, "that we turn ourselves in and go on back to Camp Trinidad to take up where we left off?" He paused. "Why, yes. I'm sure your people would willingly wipe the slate clean and forgive our 'murdering' ways."

"Oh, you misunderstand, Colonel. I'm not talkin' about you. We both know what you got waiting for you. It's your boys here I'm thinkin' of. They'll die out here 'less you throw down and come back with me. I'll see to it they get a fair hearing."

"These *boys*, as you call them, would sooner die a slow, painful death than go back to rot in that stinking camp."

"You ask 'um about that, Colonel? You put it to the vote?"

Glowering, Von Toth drew his arm up, backhanded Jack across the face, and then thrust a stiff index finger under his freshly bleeding nose. "I grow tired of your disrespect! Maybe I should just end it right here and now and be done with you!"

With new blood in the corners of his mouth, Jack glared at him. "You do what you gotta do. I stopped living the moment I put that gun to your head. I ain't expectin' nothin' except maybe the joy of seein' you take a bullet afore I go out."

Jack watched as Von Toth stared at him, his lips working, his eyes growing darker.

"You know, I never expected to meet my equal in this country, Jack Carson. You are surely a cut above anything I've come upon during my brief time here."

"Spare me the bull," snapped Jack.

Von Toth flashed what he hoped was a superior grin, and walked slowly around his adversary, studying him. "You know, Jack, we may be able to work something out here. I'd planned to release your children once we'd made it through the pass. They'd be of no use to me in New Mexico. But you—you are a different story. I can see where a man of your obvious skill and resourcefulness could be just what the doctor ordered to see me and my men safely on to the Mexican border." In front of Jack again, Von Toth engaged him eye to eye. "What do you say? Your life in exchange for seeing us to our destination. You have my word as a German officer and a gentleman that I'll release you unharmed at the Mexican border. You can be back at your fabled ranch with your loving family by week's end. Do we have a deal?"

Jack spat a thick, red gout of congealed blood onto the toe of Von Toth's boot. Feeling hard as the Rocky Mountains, angrier than he'd ever been before, he locked eyes with his tormentor. "I know a gentleman when I see one, Colonel," he said, "and you sure as hell don't fit the description. Your word ain't worth the blood I just spit on your foot. Yeah, I'll sure enough be your guide, but you ain't never gonna live to see Mexico."

Von Toth stepped back, and unleashed a mighty kick to Jack's groin.

Jack crumpled, fell, and vomited on the ground.

His features like cold marble, Von Toth wiped the blood from his boot onto the leg of Jack's jeans, and then standing, breathing hard, he spoke to Georg. "You have a new assignment here, Georg. Guard this man with your life."

Von Toth, still in a fierce heat, turned away, and when he did, Georg bent over the still retching Jack, took him by the arm and helped him to his feet. "Here," he said, and led him to Straub's horse, which was now standing saddled with the others. With difficulty, he helped the stricken man into the saddle. Jack, now astride, hands tied behind him, leaning his head against the horse's neck and mane and still spitting, watched Georg fasten a rope from the saddle horn of Jack's horse to his own.

Jack roused, lifted his head, saliva and blood and vomit dripping down his chin, and croaked. "You trying to kill us both?"

Georg stopped and stared at him. "What…?"

"Take that rope," Jack said, "make a slip knot and loop it around this horse's neck and then make a half hitch around his nose. With that, you can make him follow you, and if he gets contrary, you can choke him off." Jack extended his bound hands to help with the slip knot and half hitch.

Georg craved to offer this man the same assurance he had offered his children. He lifted a water canteen to Jack's lips.

"Georg!" bellowed Von Toth.

Georg looked around.

Von Toth's eyes were narrowed in anger as he swung himself into his saddle and rode toward them. He wrenched the canteen from Georg's hand. "We shall not waste our precious water on this wretch. And you shall do without water yourself today on account of your indiscretion. Understood?"

Georg bit his tongue. "Yes, my colonel."

Von Toth scowled at the hostage with hate-filled eyes. "Let's be on our way. You will lead us, Mr. Carson. And lead well, or I'll shoot you out of your saddle."

Jack choked down bitter rage, but only because he was determined to see this murdering mob on down into New Mexico and straight into the army ambush he knew awaited them.

◆　　　◆　　　◆

Cassie and Josh had not gone far. Sick with terror, and finding that they could not bear to leave their father alone with Von Toth, they had lain hidden less than a quarter mile from the camp. Unless they or Georg could do *some*thing, they had seen their father alive for the last time.

Less than an hour ago, Josh had crept soundlessly back to watch, and now on his return, he found Cassie, flushed and excited, looking at a piece of paper in her hand.

"Josh, look! Pa slipped this into my jeans pocket! Listen!" she began reading it aloud. "Dead end at Cougar Canyon, ten to twelve miles southwest of Raton. Take old logging road to Raton, and tell Sheriff Polk to have the army set up there later today. Should be there early evening."

"Raton! You know how to get there from here, Cassie?"

"Why, yeah. Of course. But what about *you*? You're coming with me, aren't you?"

"No. I'm riding on ahead. I can't leave Pa. Maybe I can distract 'um enough so Pa and Georg can slip away free." He paused and his gaze locked with hers. "Cassie, you gotta take that note on into Sheriff Polk at Raton. You heard what Georg said about the colonel planning to kill us once we got 'um through that pass. He ain't likely to do better by Pa. Not unless Pa can convince 'um he can help 'um on to Mexico."

Cassie placed a loving hand on her brother's arm. "OK, I'll go alone, but you be careful, Josh!"

Josh smiled and hugged his sister. "The Germans may have all the guns, but you and me and Pa hold all the high cards out here. We know this country. We got a good chance…an awful good chance!"

With her brother's words repeating in her mind, Cassie leapt to her feet, caught up the reins, mounted, and rode hard due east to reach Raton via the old logging road.

14

Sheriff Forrest Polk and his deputy, Lou Stachowiak, sat at their favorite table in the middle of the Highland Hotel's comfortable dining room. Polk had all but killed off his usual rancher's breakfast—three eggs over easy, a thick slab of hamburger steak, four pieces of whole-wheat toast dripping with butter, greasy hash browns, and steaming hot coffee heavy with sugar and cream.

Stachowiak contented himself with black coffee sweetened with brown sugar, having breakfasted with his family only a couple of hours earlier.

Polk was a big-bellied man several double-chocolate sundaes past obese. Of average height, he was in his late fifties and had a big fleshy face with a coarse complexion and wide-set eyes. A beat-up cowboy hat, sweat-stained around the band and pulled down to eyebrow level, hid his thinning, curly gray hair. Rock steady and stubborn as a mule, he'd been sheriffing in Raton for thirty-three years, starting out as a deputy and eventually settling into the sheriff's chair. He knew everybody in this town, and everybody knew him—for better or worse. He'd gotten the best of bandits and drunks, card sharks and rustlers, outbrawling the worst they could throw at him. He hadn't backed away from a good fight in all those thirty-three years, and he had the scars to prove it. The only scrap he ever lost was to a big woman he'd come to rescue from her wife-beating mate. He'd subdued her abuser with a vicious right hook, and she'd responded by knocking Polk stone-cold with a coal shovel.

Polk's wife and kids had pulled out on him years ago—she'd given him the choice: his family or his job—and he hadn't seen them since. He missed his family, but not enough to walk away from the only line of work he'd ever known. He'd never once second-guessed his decision.

Deputy Stachowiak was pretty much the exact opposite of Polk. Tall, slim-waisted—about a sugared coffee past gaunt—he was a reasonably good-looking man with a full head of jet black hair bathed in cream and combed straight back like a Denver lawyer's. A pair of horn-rimmed glasses sat on the bridge of his nose, and his narrow-brimmed Stetson rested in his lap. He was a model family man, just thirty-four years young. He did have one thing in common with his superior—an undying love for law enforcement. He'd cut his teeth in the business while battling Chicago gangsters. He'd still be in Chicago if not for his wife's insistence that he take a less warlike assignment in the country. Two years ago, he'd answered an ad to relocate to peaceful Raton, New Mexico, and since then, had pretty much fallen in love with the town.

Their waitress, Candace, stopped to refill their coffee cups. Polk's age, she'd waitressed here nearly twenty years. Long and leggy, she was heavily made up with painted red fingernails and toes, and she spoke with a brittle, tobacco-roughened voice.

Polk swatted her backside. "Atta girl, Candy. Thought you'd given us up for dead over here."

"My husband catches you swatting me like that, Sheriff, and he'd be liable to take no notice of that badge you're wearing. He'll teach you to be cheeky with me."

"Darling, I already know how to be cheeky with you. Left and right cheek, makes no difference."

The dining room's manager and chief cook, Charlie Rodgers, sauntered over to engage his most respected patron. A tall, slim, mustachioed man with smooth, wet-plastered hair combed across a balding skull, he said with a smile, "Forrest, what you need is to marry up with one of those well-off Smithson spinsters just outta town. Give you something of your own to swat at."

"You had a good look at those old girls in the full light of day, Charlie? I'd give 'um a two, and that's only cause I ain't never seen a one before. Wasn't it you once told me your customers take the first bite with their eyes? I tell you, it ain't no different with the fairer sex. If you don't like what you're looking at, you're never gonna see it through, no matter how much money they got or how good a pot stew they make."

"And how about you, Sheriff?" inquired Candace in a sardonic tone. "What you think those Smithson girls figure they're looking at when they're eyeballing *you*? Clark Gable?"

"Hey, Candy. I ain't saying I'm pretty to look at," Polk raised his hands in defense. "But you can't argue I got a certain *seductiveness*. There's just something I give off, natural like."

"It's called body odor," chortled Stachowiak. "Take a bath."

While the others chuckled at his expense, Polk again swatted Candace on the backside. "To tell you the truth, boys, I'm just biding my time waiting for old Warren to kick off so I can hitch up with Candy here."

Candace forged a smile. "I'd sooner put a gun in my mouth."

"A woman with spunk. I like that," said Polk. "Come on. Admit it, girl. It's gotta be comforting knowing there's single studs like me around in case old Warren goes toes up on you."

Candace good-naturedly shoved Polk's hat down over his eyes and ambled off, muttering, "In your dreams."

"I gotta get back at it," said Charlie as he started for the kitchen. "You men have yourselves a fine day."

Polk readjusted his hat, washed down a mouthful of toast with one last swig of coffee, and playfully called out, "And no more mixing dog meat in with the hamburger, Charlie. You hear? I'll shut you down! I swear!"

An old-timer on his way to the till slapped Polk on the arm and asked, "How's it going, Sheriff?"

Polk grinned and replied, "Well, nobody's taken a shot at me yet, Clem. Thanks for asking."

Old Clem chuckled. "Yeah, but the day's young, Sheriff."

Polk waved him good-bye and said to his deputy, "Well, Lou, my man, I suspect we ought a go earn our keep, or at least make it look that way."

Stachowiak led the way to the till with a bowlegged stride.

Polk laid a hand on his deputy's shoulder. "If I die before you, Lou old buddy, I swear I'm gonna leave you my legs in my will so's you don't have to walk around on those two anymore."

Candace waved them off. "It's on me today, boys. Have yourselves a good one."

"Why, that's mighty Christian of you, Candy!" exclaimed Polk.

"Listen, Forrest," she said. "Warren's been after me to have you over for dinner. Tonight OK with you?"

"Tonight's just fine, less I get lucky with one of those Smithson girls in the meantime."

Candace chuckled. "See you tonight."

Polk and his deputy made for the door. Polk said, "Now, you see. Swat 'um on the behind, flatter 'um up a bit. Free breakfast, free dinner—works like a charm."

15

It was a heavily overcast morning, an ocean of ragged gray clouds having moved in from the north, and the first bitter winds of a coming storm descended upon Raton. The two lawmen had just crossed the street en route to their office when they saw coming toward them, a frazzled teenaged girl.

Cassie's troubled blue eyes locked on Polk's badge. Her voice was strained, her words a near incoherent babble. "Sheriff Polk?"

"For a fact. What can I do for you, girly?"

"My pa! The Germans have him!"

Dumbfounded, Polk squinted his eyes. "Come again?" he said.

"German POWs. From Camp Trinidad! They killed my aunt and uncle, and they've got my pa! They're gonna kill him too!"

"Your pa?"

"Jack Carson!"

"The escaped German prisoners of war!" Stachowiak said. "The ones that didn't turn up for work at the Segundo Coal Mines and killed their two guards. I was gonna tell you at the office, Forrest. When I opened up this morning there was an urgent wire from Camp Trinidad warning us to be on the lookout for some runaway POWs possibly coming our way."

"That's them. Nine or ten men," Cassie said. "All armed to the teeth with weapons from our ranch. They're heading to Cougar Canyon, and they've forced my pa to lead them. He said to have you tell the army to wait there for them sometime early this evening."

Stachowiak broke into a run toward the sheriff's office down the street.

Polk removed his hat and ran a hand through his sparse crop. "Heavily armed German soldiers on their way to Cougar Canyon?"

"That's right, Sheriff," she answered.

"Well, from what I know of your pa, young lady, those Germans have theirselves badly outnumbered. But you can count on us taking care of everything from here on. You look like you could use some tending to yourself. Now you go on across to the Highland Hotel. Lady named Candace works in the diner there. You tell her I said to fix you up with some food and a room."

"No, sir! Thank you, sir, but I can't stop! I gotta get on to Cougar Canyon to wait for my pa." She turned on her heels but Polk stopped her.

"Young lady, I can't let you do that." He walked to within arm's length of her and looked her in the eyes. "Listen," he said. "I know you *wanta* go out there. But you could get yourself killed, and just as bad, your bein' there could get some other folks killed. I hate to pull rank on you, but I'm gonna have to." He paused. "Now, if you don't come along, I'll *make* you come."

Cassie stood a moment looking at him. She was desperate to run, but she knew there was no use. With anger and bitter tears, she nodded, and they crossed the street together.

◆   ◆   ◆

Having left the Carson girl with Candice, Polk marched to the office, where Deputy Stachowiak had just gotten off the phone to Camp Trinidad.

"I told 'um about Carson's plan for Cougar Canyon," he said. "The army's got one big bug up their butt over this Colonel Von Toth and his boys. Jack Carson's oldest boy is guiding the army in a search somewhere between here and the pass."

With his left hand on his hip, Polk picked at his teeth with the nail of his right index finger, his mind abuzz. "Lou, we're gonna need a good-sized posse to ride the high country. You drive out to Bob Barton's west of town. See how many horses he can have saddled and ready to go by twelve noon."

"You aren't thinking of going after those POWs?"

"You bet your sweet ass I am. You know how many good families lie right in the path of those murdering Nazis? We can have those boys rounded up and in my jail by suppertime tonight."

"Sheriff, there aren't but a handful of ranches out that way. You and I can drive out ourselves to warn them to vacate their properties. Ain't no need to risk our lives going after trained German soldiers when half the U.S. Army's gonna be waiting for 'um just down the road at Cougar Canyon."

Polk's eyes flashed, and his tone was final. "You do as I say, deputy, and drive out to the Barton's and help him saddle up twenty to thirty head of horses. I'll be along within the hour with a like number of men."

"But, Forrest, the *army*…"

Polk slammed a fist down on the desk and thundered, "The army don't know crap about this country. This is *my* turf. I've ridden every square inch of that path they gotta take to reach Cougar Canyon; I know it like the back of my hand. Now, either get with the program or turn in that badge."

Stunned, Stachowiak stared at his superior with squinted eyes. Mouth agape, he lifted his hands in protest. "Forrest, *listen* to me! I've got a gut chock-full of bad instincts about this! You telling me I'm done here if I refuse a part in this insanity?"

"The choice is yours. I thought you of all people would want to hunt down these escaped Nazis after what they done to your native Poland."

"Yeah, I got my reasons for hating the Germans. But I just can't see the point in a lot of good townsfolk risking their lives when the U.S. Army already has a plan in place to take them down. I ain't scared for myself. I've faced worse on the streets of Chicago more times than I care to remember, but I got a wife and four kids to think of."

"All right then," Polk said. "You can stay home and keep your job to boot. Just drive out to Barton's for me and help saddle up those horses. I got a posse to round up. There are men in this town who don't take kindly to enemy soldiers prancing around in their backyards. Tell me—how you gonna feel if one of our people stumbles into those Nazi thugs between now and when the army sets up their ambush at Cougar Canyon? We're responsible, Lou—responsible for the welfare of every man, woman, and child in this entire county.

"Besides, I ain't about to do anything foolish out there. We'll just sit and wait at the Ram Falls fishing hole just west of town. Carson's sure to lead 'um there to water the horses. I'll have so many guns trained on those poor sons-a-guns, they won't know whether to break wind or sing the national anthem." He paused to think, then said, "Lou, I know how you feel toward your family, so I'll leave it to you. But you swore an oath to protect these good people. You been under fire before, and that's more than I can say for any of the boys I'll be recruiting. I really need you out there, but you decide." Polk turned to leave. "Just be sure you and the Bartons have our mounts ready at noon. OK?"

Stachowiak felt suddenly ashamed. And he felt himself yielding, bending like a sapling in a strong wind. His face grew tight. "OK, Sheriff, I'll be joining you, but I hope for our sakes we're not carrying home some of these good posse men strapped across their saddles."

Polk stopped at the door, a wide grin on his face. "We'll all be coming back, Lou. You've got my word on that. I'll see you at Barton's."

Minutes later, Stachowiak was headed west in his 1935 Ford pickup truck with faded black paint and a million miles on it. He had one stop to make en route to the Barton Ranch; he wanted to tell Marianne he'd be home late. He also needed that Thompson submachine gun that had kept him safe on the bloody streets of Chicago. Upon leaving the force, his captain had made the Thompson an under-the-table gift to him for twelve years of service to the city. He wondered how he'd break the news of his pursuit of the German POWs to Marianne. But then again, should he even tell her?

Maybe Sheriff Polk's going after the POWs wasn't such a bad idea after all. These men had killed already and could kill again before the army's planned apprehension at Cougar Canyon. They had to be stopped.

Stachowiak parked in his driveway and skipped up the stairs to his house, still wondering how he'd explain this. The house was empty. A glance out the kitchen window revealed Marianne working in the garden and the kids playing nearby. No need to explain the Thompson to Marianne. They'd been married seven years, and this kind of thing worried her. He dashed upstairs, got it off the top shelf of the closet, and rushed it back to the car.

A light rain was falling as he made his way around to the backyard, calling out, "Hey, honey!"

Marianne turned to greet him. "Hi! What are you doing home?"

"Just had to pick something up," he replied, a touch of guilt in his voice. "Listen, I…I'm gonna be late tonight. Gotta go out of town with Sheriff Polk."

"Something serious?" asked Marianne.

"No, hon, nothing serious." He pecked at her forehead and embraced her. He then reached to tousle his oldest son's hair and glanced at the younger ones playing in the sandbox.

His wife stopped and leaned on the hoe handle, looking at him. The apprehension in Lou's face was a dead giveaway; she recognized it every time. Marianne crossed her arms and took on the look of someone who had been lied to. "Lou, what is it?"

"What?"

"We've known one another far too long to play these games."

He hung his head and reached to take her arms in his strong hands. His words were almost a whisper. "I didn't want you worrying, sweetheart. Some German soldiers escaped from Camp Trinidad up in Colorado yesterday. They're headed this way. The sheriff's forming a posse, and we're riding up after them into the high country this afternoon."

"But isn't that the *army's* concern?"

"Yes, yes it is. But, these men have already killed some folks back in Colorado, and Sheriff Polk's afraid they'll kill again before the army can see to them."

Marianne's pretty blue eyes began to tear. "We're never gonna escape it, are we, Lou? One day I'll be burying you on account of that cursed badge."

"No, honey. The sheriff gave me his word—nothing reckless. Any gunplay and I'll be out of there like a cut cat."

"Don't lie to me, Lou Stachowiak. Any gunplay and you'll be into it up to your neck."

Lou looked away; Marianne was dead right. It wasn't in him to run from a fight.

"We can leave this place, Lou. We can go away and start a new life. You weren't born a lawman, you know. You can get another job to feed your family."

They'd been down this road too many times, and Lou wasn't having any of it. "Marianne, I love you and the children more than anything in this world, but I took an oath to protect these people, and I gotta see it through."

As Lou pecked her on the cheek, Marianne wiped a tear and turned away to plant her corn.

He turned and headed back to his pick up. Sheriff Polk and his posse were counting on him to have those horses ready to go.

16

Ram Falls, a spectacular sight a mere two-hour horseback ride from Raton, was not like most falls where the water suddenly drops off a sheer ledge to a still pool below. Ram Falls was a series of short falls, like stair steps. Hikers and trail riders came here often; hunters and fishermen came by the hundreds.

A slow, soaking rain had blown in from the north, leaving the land wet and green and smelling of spring. The sky, heavy and cold and gray, lay well below the mountaintops, hiding the peaks. Thick mists, heavy laden with moisture, drifted down between the ridges. All was hushed and eerie…made eerier by intermittent thunder that now and again burst like cannon fire overhead.

The falls were enclosed on one side of the river by towering cliffs. On the other side sat Sheriff Polk and the bulk of his Raton posse.

With the falls before them, the cliffs to their right, and Polk's men waiting in ambush on the left, Von Toth and his men would have no choice but to surrender. Or so the sheriff had said. Their only way out was straight back the way they'd come, and Polk would plug that leak with a half dozen of his finest men, including battle-tested Deputy Stachowiak.

The Raton posse, twenty-three men strong, was a mix of old and young, some skilled with a hunting rifle and others not, ploughboys who'd never fired at a human being, shopkeepers who'd never held a rifle, teenaged young men caught up in a spirit of adventure. The group included a couple of army reserves, a banker, a lawyer, and a preacher. Some were scared spitless; others were thrilled at the prospect of doing battle with the hated Hitlerites.

Polk counted on sheer strength of numbers to persuade the POWs to throw down and come back peacefully. For all his bluster, the sheriff sure knew his stuff. The posse hadn't been settled into their posts a half hour when they got their first glimpse of Jack Carson leading his German captors straight to the falls.

◆   ◆   ◆

With cold rain dripping from his hat, Jack Carson was nearing exhaustion. His nerves were frayed, and his stomach was close to mutiny. They had come over and down Raton Pass and were now about two hours inside New Mexico, and the falls below were in sight.

They had been on the trail a little more than an hour when Von Toth had seen it was impossible for Jack to ride any further with his hands tied behind him, and had ordered Georg to cut him loose. It'd taken a good fifteen minutes of flexing his fingers before the feeling came back, but come back it had, and that with a vengeance. Since then, off and on, Jack had ridden with his eyes closed in prayer. He sensed death itself hunting him down, and he was thinking mostly of how to spare Wade and Josh and Cassie the agony of his death.

Now he heard Colonel Von Toth riding up even with him, and Jack turned his head slightly.

"This is the fresh water you spoke of, Mr. Carson?" Von Toth said, nodding toward the falls and the river below.

Jack nodded. "Last fresh water we'll see till morning. Better let the horses rest and drink before pushing on. There's a cave this side of the river bank; we can shelter down in it out of the rain."

"Fine. Lead us there."

The rain was heavy now as they came down the narrow trail single-file, and at the river's edge, followed it along the base of a sheer rock wall that reached up several hundred feet. The wall's weathered granite was dark and damp, and here and there, little rivulets crossed the trail, wetting the horses' hooves to the fetlocks as they passed across. The light was sparse, dimmed by the heavy clouds and the depth of the escarpment.

The POWs, hunted beasts adrift in misery, followed like sheep. At last, the mouth of the cave yawned before them, and all in a line, they ducked their heads and rode into the darkness, the clop of the horses's hooves echoing from the walls and low ceiling. Soaked through to the skin, legs and backs aching, they dismounted and listened in the quietness to the rush of the falls, and to the unyielding rain striking the ground outside and dripping from the entrance.

◆   ◆   ◆

Deputy Stachowiak and five posse men scrambled from their wooded shelter to take up positions dead center in the path of the POW's would-be retreat.

"Fish in a barrel," said Polk to Charlie Rodgers as the two sat together observing the dismounted German soldiers leading their horses out to water at the river's edge.

"You think they'll throw down?" asked Charlie.

"Yes, I do. Wouldn't have brought you boys out here otherwise. I'm going on down to talk some sense into 'um." Polk unbuckled his holster, laid it beside his rifle, and fastened a white handkerchief to a stick.

"You take care, Forrest," said Charlie.

"I plan to do just that."

White flag in hand, Polk clumsily made his way down the steep, rain-slick bank toward the river.

◆   ◆   ◆

Standing just inside the cave's mouth, gazing out through the curtain of rain, Jack saw the portly figure descending the far bank and recognized it as Polk.

"Crazy fool," he muttered.

"You know this man?" asked Georg.

"Yeah, I know him," Jack replied.

As Polk reached the bottom of the bank and waded into the swift but shallow waters at the base of the falls, Jack called out to him.

"Polk, you damned fool! *Go back!*"

The colonel came to the cave's mouth. "Shut up, Carson," he growled. "Let him come."

Jack wondered if in the rain's roar, Polk had heard him. Heard him or not, he kept coming; he climbed the gentle rise, and standing a few feet outside the cave, his legs wet from the river, the rain running off his hat down onto the shoulders of his slicker, Polk came face to face with the German colonel who had led the breakout.

The two men stood regarding each other.

"You the colonel?" Polk said, raising his voice over the sound of the rain. His breath was short from his climb down the bank and his wading the rock-bottomed river.

Von Toth took a formal military step forward. "I am Colonel Helmut Von Toth of the German *Wehrmacht*, sir. And you?"

"Sheriff Forrest Polk of Raton, New Mexico," he said. "Now, you boys would do well to throw down your firearms and come on in peaceful. You got no way outta here, and the army's on its way. We can wait you out if we have to."

Polk saw Von Toth's eyes turn up toward the trees on the height beyond the river, and heard him say,

"May I ask the size of your force, Sheriff?"

"I got twenty-two men, Colonel." He pointed up across the river. "Most are up in the trees there lookin' down on ya. Another half dozen are mindin' your path of retreat outta here—should you be so foolish."

"Well, it would appear you have the upper hand, sir."

"Darn rights! You got, what, nine men here? That's twenty-three to nine. Pretty bad odds, I'd say."

"I assure you, Sheriff Polk, my men and I would have it no other way. We're quite at home with such odds."

As Polk gazed at Von Toth's face, hard as wood, eyes set and cold, he saw Von Toth's hand moving, and Polk felt his own breath stop.

Slowly, Von Toth drew his pistol. "But maybe I should reduce those odds just a bit," he said.

Polk stared at the drawn weapon. He'd never been afraid—not truly afraid—of anything in his life, until this moment. He felt the blood drain from his face, and suddenly he knew he was a ruined man. His heart pounded, and there was the dagger-like stab of fear in his belly. Polk lifted his gaze from the gun's muzzle to the colonel's eyes just as the pistol discharged.

Jack Carson saw Polk stumble backward, fall, and lie still in the pounding rain, his head in the edge of the rushing river.

◆   ◆   ◆

Up the trail, across the only path the POWs could take out of this canyon, Lou Stachowiak heard the gunshot, watched Polk fall, and knew that his gut had told him the truth; there would be lots more blood spilled this day. "They'll be coming this way, boys," he said. "Hold your fire till you've got a kill shot."

◆   ◆   ◆

Von Toth turned to Georg at the back of the dimly lit cave and spoke in a voice cold as death. "Shoot your prisoner, Georg. The rest of you mount up and get ready to breakout."

With pounding heart, Georg looked into the face of Jack Carson. Whatever happens, he thought, he could not end this good man's life. But he slowly drew the revolver from his belt, never taking his eyes off Jack's eyes that were now staring back at him. Georg drew back the hammer, tightened on the trigger, and fired wide of Jack. The sound in the confines of the cave deafened him and his ears rang so that he could hear nothing.

Jack, also deafened but astonished to be alive, did not need to be told what to do. Instantly, he crumpled to the cave floor and lay still.

Georg tucked the pistol back into his belt and looked up to see the others mounting up for what he knew was an insane life-or-death flight for freedom. He was, he was certain, moments from his own death, and there was absolutely nothing he could do about it. But at least, he thought, death would deliver him from his mental and emotional anguish, from the guilt of having become a thug and a killer. *God have mercy on my soul*, he prayed, and ducking his head beneath the cave's low ceiling, mounted his horse. At the cave's mouth, Von Toth addressed his men with fierce, desperate words. "Comrades, there's no going back! We've left a trail of blood the Americans will never forgive us for. Have your weapons at the ready."

He abruptly reined his horse around and spurred out into the still hard-driving rain.

His heart heavy, Georg nudged the sides of his mount and followed. With lightning flashing over his head, and thunder rolling down the narrow canyon, and the sharp crack of rifle fire aloft as the Raton posse unleashed its vengeance, Georg crouched low and watched a comrade fall from his saddle to the wet rocky earth. Only a few feet outside the cave, the horse of the man just ahead of him fell, and when Georg swung down and had grabbed his arm to help him, another bullet caught the man, killing him. Instantly, another fusillade brought down *Georg's* horse, forcing him back into the cave as bullets kicked up bits of rock about him. At the cave's entrance, one took a bite out of Georg's side, and sent him sprawling in.

Moments before, certain the cave had emptied, Jack had gotten to his feet and was peering out at the mayhem when Georg came rolling in and lay still at his feet. Quickly, Jack picked him up and carried him deeper into the cave.

◆   ◆   ◆

Stachowiak and his men, stationed behind low boulders that flanked the trail, were astonished to see that a half-dozen men and horses had survived the onslaught and now were riding straight toward them.

His heart a runaway train, Stachowiak watched them thundering up the narrow trail. He felt beads of sweat trickle into his eyes, stinging and blurring his vision. "All right!" he shouted. "Prepare to fire!" Tense, he hugged the Thompson submachine gun close under his right arm, finger on the trigger. "Let 'um *have* it, boys!" he hollered. Their rifles boomed, and the rapid tommy gun fire sounded like ripping paper.

But on the Germans came, responding with pistol fire that kicked up bits of rock at Stachowiak's feet. The man next to him went down, and he heard another shout, "I didn't sign up for no shootin' match with the German Army!" And the man bolted for cover.

"*Hold* 'um!" cried Stachowiak who was now firing short, aimed bursts. "Stand and fight, damn you! Stand and fight!"

But the others broke and ran for it.

Stachowiak fired a long sweeping burst that knocked two men from their mounts. Rock fragments kicked up in front of him, and he spun to his left to take up a better position. Von Toth was bearing down, and Stachowiak turned the Thompson upon him, but a second too late. A bullet from the colonel's pistol smashed into his forehead and his body spun and fell to the rocky ground below.

With that, a sudden calm embraced the landscape, the only sounds now were the pounding rain and the thunder and the hooves of horses as Von Toth and two of his men rode hard for the sheltering woods.

17

In the dark shelter of the cave, Jack examined Georg's wound, tucked his folded gloves beneath the man's head and spread his coat over the trembling body. "You're gonna be all right, son," he said quietly. "We'll get you some help."

"Thank...you," Georg answered, his eyes rolling back in shock.

"You tell 'um when they come for you that you're my hired man. You hear? Call yourself, Dave...Dave Mankowski. OK?"

"OK."

Lifting the coat, Jack unbuckled Georg's pistol belt, covered him again, and fastened it to his own waist. He drew the revolver, opened the loading gate, hauled the hammer back to half cock, and turned the cylinder. Forty-five caliber, all chambers full, but three of the shiny brass heads were marked with the tell-tale dent that told him only three live cartridges remained. He closed the loading gate, turned the cylinder so the next round was ready, lowered the hammer, and shoved the pistol into the holster.

This thing's far from over, he thought. He had watched Von Toth and two others escape the trap. Left free, they'd continue their murder and mayhem all the way to the Mexican border.

Jack placed a warm hand on Georg's forehead. "I'll see they take good care of you. Remember, your name's Dave Mankowski, my ranch hand. Got it?"

Georg managed a weak, compliant smile. Through dry lips that peeled apart as he spoke, "Dave Mankowski," he repeated.

Jack rose from his knees knowing that with better than a dozen trigger-happy vigilantes up on the ridge, he couldn't break out of this cave unannounced. He took a deep breath and stepped toward the gray light and falling rain, but stayed just inside, out of sight. Cupping both hands around his mouth, he yelled slowly and with all his lungs's might, "Hold your fire! The name's Jack Carson! I'm coming out!" He waited. Nothing. Then he called again. At last a voice answered through the thunder and rain—a long, thin yell.

"Jack!" the voice called. "It's Charlie Rodgers. You all right?"

Jack moved out into the rain leading his horse. He lifted his gaze to the ridge, where three men made small by the distance emerged from the timber, and one he recognized as Rodgers. Jack waited until another roar of thunder subsided, then cupping his hands and filling his lungs again, shouted across the river, "I'm fine, Charlie! Listen…I got a wounded man down here. One of my ranch hands from over at Segundo. See to him, would you, Charlie? I'm going after the Germans!"

The voice came back, "You got it, Jack!"

And Jack saw Charlie waving him on.

Jack bent and grabbed a rifle from the wet ground at his feet and looked at it in surprise. It was his favorite elk gun, his Remington bolt action .270, a cartridge that shot flat and hard and true. He checked the sights to see they hadn't been knocked out of line. They hadn't. He checked the chamber; it was empty, then the magazine. Four live rounds left. Four soft nosed, high powered cartridges. With the pistol, a total of seven shots—no more, no less. He'd have to choose his targets well. Satisfied, he swung into the wet, creaking saddle to pursue Von Toth, who by now had a long head start on him. "But I know the country and the colonel doesn't," he said to himself, "and that gives me the upper hand."

Spurred on by a furious bonfire of revenge burning inside, remembering Cassie and Josh and his four hunting friends, and remembering the Koivunens and Trapper Anderson, Jack rode full out through the rain and up the narrow trail. Under heavy skies and rolling thunder, he crossed the river and climbed the mountainside into the Ponderosa and aspen forest. Now riding ahead, he kept a watch for branches, and at the same time, for the disturbed ground that was sure to lead him deep into the New Mexican wild.

◆   ◆   ◆

Jack had been riding for an hour now, and the path was becoming clearer. He knew the area well, and he knew that the POWs path would soon cut a road headed south toward an abandoned mine. Von Toth wouldn't know about the mine, but any road that looked like it was headed south, he would be bound to take. And Jack knew a shortcut through miles of clear-cut trees. Within another twenty minutes, he reached the road and saw through the rain, in the dim, gray distance, three riders.

As Jack left the grass and trees for the road, he saw that the riders had stopped; they were watching their back trail and had seen him already.

◆   ◆   ◆

Von Toth's upper lip quivered as he watched the man ride up onto the road. Were his eyes deceiving him? The man had Jack *Carson's* likeness. Hadn't Carson been shot dead back in the cave? *Georg!* Von Toth uttered a fierce German curse. The backstabber had left the mountain man alive!

Von Toth formed his plan. The old road was about to take a sharp left bend among trees and abrupt hillocks—ideal for an ambush. He motioned to his men and, together, they rode on. After rounding the steeply ascending bend, he signaled them to dismount, and they found shelter in the rain-drenched foliage and among the boulders that lined the road.

It was only moments later when he heard the distinctive, rapid thud of horse hooves striking the road and rounding the bend. The colonel smiled to himself as he leveled his carbine; he was about to end his ongoing feud with the fabled Jack Carson. The smile on his face died—died at the spectacle of a riderless horse galloping his way.

◆   ◆   ◆

Jack had made a running dismount and sprinted soundlessly through the dense woodland gorse. Many a time he'd outfoxed the shrewdest of God's creatures and come away with their hides, and he'd not fail today.

He heard Von Toth bark the order to "Mount up!" and then, from just beyond the rise, came the sound of hurried footsteps.

Jack reached the crest but couldn't make out the POWs through the dense growth, but one horse and soon another came into sight across the road.

A shot from Jack's revolver echoed in the trees. Then another, and another—three shots, each one kicking up mud at each horse's heels, stampeding them headlong down the rutted road. He shoved the gun back into its holster; one, two, three; the pistol rounds were gone. He raised the rifle before him.

And now the POWs were shooting back. A bullet thudded into a tree trunk at Jack's elbow, another cut a limb over his head and it brushed his shoulder as it fell.

"Cover!" barked Von Toth, and Jack heard the men scurrying for shelter.

Jack ran again, low, swift but soundless, flanking his adversaries, coming between them and the stampeded horses, which had now slowed to a trot downhill.

◆   ◆   ◆

Josh, who had too much Carson in him to run from a fight, had been trailing the POWs all day, waiting for his chance. He'd come upon Ram Falls just as his pa, on horseback, had disappeared into the trees across the river and up the mountainside, and Josh had lit out after him. Keyed up, his young blood running hot, he'd gained on his dad enough to see him enter the road in back of the renegades, and then he'd heard the gunfire. With heated determination, he burst down the logging road in full flight. Though unarmed, he couldn't stand by with his dad in a deadly gun battle.

◆   ◆   ◆

Von Toth whispered the order, "Karl, you, come in around him from the left. Dreibach, do the same on the right."

He watched Dreibach run crouching, until a rifle shot rang out, and Dreibach fell. From where Von Toth stood, he could see from Dreibach's bloody shirt that he'd been shot clean through the heart.

Incredible marksmanship! thought Von Toth.

Von Toth glanced up and saw Jack's horse now standing a stone's throw away. "Cover me!" he whispered to Karl Weber, and crawled back through the sheltering brush toward the animal.

The sound of something falling in the brush behind him, made Von Toth glance back; then a shot thundered, and Von Toth saw Weber hurled back in among the trees.

In panic, Von Toth bolted, stumbled, caught the saddle horn of the horse, and a moment later was galloping wildly back in the direction from which he'd come. With Carson afoot, he could now break free.

From behind him, he heard another thunderous boom, felt his right arm go numb and limp, heard his rifle clatter to the roadway. He looked down and gasped at the gaping exit wound in his shoulder.

But Von Toth spurred the horse on, and rounding the bend found himself on a collision course with a young man whose face he knew—a young man riding hell-bent-for-leather toward him. The colonel tried to reach for the pistol at his side, but his shoulder and arm, stunned numb, would have none of it.

Their horses collided, and Von Toth was horrified to see Josh leap toward him, to feel his arms close around him, the weight of his body dragging him from the saddle and into the air. Falling with the boy on top of him, Von Toth's back hit hard on the roadway, and he felt the wind knocked out of him. At the same instant, from the corner of his eye, he saw his pistol fly out and land in the slick, red mud of the ditch. He was desperate to breathe, but he could not do it.

With a savage thrust, Von Toth pushed the boy off, hurried to his feet, and swung madly with his right boot, delivered a glancing blow to his adversary's head. He lunged for the pistol, but incredibly, the boy was up again and rushing toward him, head down. The head drove into his belly, and once again, Von Toth's wind was gone. They were rolling in the mud now, Von Toth struggling to see through the rain that filled his eyes. His shoulder now raged with pain, but he fought like a bull dog in a pit fights for his life. Suddenly they were on their feet again, the boy glaring at him with a fierce rage. And then Von Toth saw it, his pistol within reach of his left hand.

Von Toth grabbed up the weapon and as the boy came lunging, charging like a mad bull, Von Toth leveled the weapon at him and began squeezing the trigger. Just as the boy reached him, the crash of a shot filled the air.

For a desperate, breathless moment, Josh Carson lay atop the man, his ears ringing from the shot. He was wondering where the bullet had hit him, wondering why he felt no pain, and wondering why Von Toth lay so still. Then he glanced up and saw his father standing with rifle in hand some fifty yards away.

Josh looked back down on Von Toth and saw in the man's left temple, a small neat hole, and that the right side of his head had been blown away.

In the bone-chilling rain, Josh rose from off his enemy's dead body, and father and son slogged heavily through the deep red mud of the old log road into one another's waiting arms.

18

Georg lay propped on pillows in his hospital room in Raton. The window was open, and the smell of wonderful woodland perfume flowed in on a light breeze.

Charlie Rodgers, chief cook at the Highland Hotel and Jack Carson's friend, had brought him in late yesterday afternoon, and on the way had told "Dave Mankowski," who was weak from blood loss and weary from his grueling days on horseback, that "all twelve of those bloody German POWs" now lay dead; as—again in Rodger's words—"they sure as hell deserve to be."

The town of Raton, so Georg heard, was mourning the loss of three good men: Sheriff Forrest Polk, Deputy Lou Stachowiak, and a shopkeeper and father of three, who was new to town last month.

He'd also learned that back in Segundo, the man they called big Donny Ruck, one of the four caught in Sergeant Straub's ambush, would lose his left arm. *Ruck*, he thought, *was lucky*.

With so many dead, Georg wondered as he lay here, *why am I still alive?* These thoughts kept swirling in his mind, but now, the shot the nurse had just given him to keep down the pain was beginning to take affect, and he was feeling very relaxed and the thoughts were fading.

◆　　　◆　　　◆

It was close to noon when a sound-asleep Georg (or Dave Mankowski, as he was known here) woke up to see guests coming through his door. One by one, the Carson family was filing in.

Jack removed his Stetson and sat on the bed at Georg's side. Wade, Josh, and Cassie stood around the bed, Cassie closest, and Georg realized that her hand was touching his. This is wonderful, he thought, and smiled up at her.

He turned his head and looked at Jack, who was standing on the other side of the bed smiling down on him.

"Mornin', Georg," Jack said, and the two clasped hands.

"Mr. Carson," Georg said as he tightened his grip.

"Georg," said Jack, "I want you to meet my oldest son, Wade. Wade, this young man is the sole reason I am alive today."

With moist eyes, Wade reached to shake Georg's hand. "I'm grateful for what you done for my pa," he said.

Georg, who hadn't felt close to anybody since the German Army had torn him from his home in Stuttgart, lay there, drinking it in. These people gathered around his bed felt to him like an island of peace in a vast ocean of calamity. What could he say?

He considered each face in turn, and then said what had been burning on his mind. "I want you to know," he said in that baritone voice that surprised Cassie every time she heard it, "that we're not all like Colonel Helmut Von Toth." Georg would not belabor the point, but he would make sure they knew. "I *swear* to you," he said, "that we were following orders." No one spoke. "And yet," he clinched his jaw, and then continued, "I am as much to blame as my colonel."

At that, Jack interrupted. "No you're not, son," he said. "You did what you had to do to stay alive, and along the way, whenever you could manage it, you helped. You saved my bacon, and Josh and Cassie told me what you done for them. No man—no *father*—could ask for more."

Georg gazed at him, thinking that Jack Carson had the biggest heart of any man he had ever known. "That may be," Georg said hesitantly, "but..."

"It's over now, Georg." Jack gripped Georg's arm for emphasis. "We won't listen to anymore talk about you bein' to blame." With the hat in his hand, Jack made a sweeping motion that included all those around the bed. "Not a one of us wants to hear more. In fact, we're gonna get you outta here and on back to the ranch just as soon as they'll release you to us. They seem to have bought my story, and I really could use a good man, Georg. You can live out the war in peace on the ranch, and then, when it's over, go your own way if you want."

Georg Dreschler was not used to being the center of attention. His gaze flitted around to each face, until it lighted on Cassie's eyes and then it remained there a long moment. Smiling, he turned back to face Jack and said quietly, firmly, "Mr. Carson...how would you Americans say it? 'I'll just take you up on that deal.'"

The words sounded strange coming from the mouth of the young German, and the laughter didn't die away until the door swung open, and their collective heart chilled.

Standing in the doorway was an American army officer—a tall, well-built, silver-haired gentleman with fine features—cap in hand.

"Captain Howard MacLean, camp commandant at Trinidad," he said, and stepped toward the bed. "You must be Jack Carson."

Jack stood and extended his right hand along with an uncertain smile and a feeling of disquiet. "Yes, sir. And these are my children—Wade, Cassie, and Josh."

The officer warmly received the handshake, saying, "I'm well acquainted with your son Wade, Mr. Carson. He and I shared a frustrating day in the saddle together following those runaways." He paused and looked Jack in the eyes. "Your fine reputation precedes you, sir, and the army regrets the misery you and yours have suffered these past days. You have my assurance that you'll never be bothered again by *any* of our POWs."

The captain's steel blue eyes shifted to Georg who was lying there almost breathless, waiting for the axe to fall. The two men gazed at each other's familiar face.

Georg had served him as translator back at Trinidad these last months.

Jack watched, his eyes shifting from one man to the other and back again. Finally, he said, "Captain MacLean, allow me to introduce you to my farmhand, Dave Mankowski. As you can see, he came out of all this a little worse for wear than the rest of us did."

MacLean looked down on Georg with a stony expression. "Strange," he said. "This man bears a distinct resemblance to Georg from Camp Trinidad. He was not among the dead POWs we've come upon. Any chance you could be mistaken?"

"Why, no, sir," Jack said, "Not a chance in the world. This is Dave Mankowski."

"'Mankowski.' Why not 'Smith' or 'Jones'? Wouldn't that have been easier?"

Jack's response was a stubborn glare and a slight, meaningful smile.

MacLean addressed Georg. "Good morning, Georg. You seem to be a bit off course here."

Georg set his jaw and said nothing.

The captain turned to Jack. "Mr. Carson, could I ask that your children leave the room so that we might speak in private?"

A simple glance from their father was enough to cause Wade, Cassie, and Josh to make their way into the hall. The troubled expressions on their faces spoke of their misgivings for young Georg's future.

The captain sauntered over to the window and, with his hands behind his back, peered out. In a distant tone, he said, "Mr. Carson, let me say first that harboring an escaped prisoner of war is a hanging offense in this country. You should be very thankful I'm here to keep you from making a grave mistake. I don't know what your motive could possibly be in hiding this man from us, but I assure you, it's a foolhardy thing to do."

Wordlessly, Jack ambled around the foot of the bed and joined MacLean at the window where he, too, looked out on the morning.

"Captain," he said, "these past couple of days I've been beat up, shot at, and otherwise subjected to a hell on earth over the welfare of my children in a way you can't even begin to imagine. So don't go trying to scare me with threats to hang me. This young man saved my life and put his own on the line to save my two youngest from that sick son of a gun that you let walk off from your prison."

MacLean interrupted. "Mr. Carson, your feelings for this man don't change the fact that he's an escaped prisoner of war. Now, I'll give you folks five minutes to say thank you and good-bye. I'm putting him under guard during his stay here and will presently see him back to Camp Trinidad where he belongs."

From his bed, Georg listened to this word battle with both hope and resignation. He saw Jack clinch his jaw and look MacLean dead in the eye.

Jack said, "The army'll hang him for Von Toth's crimes, sure as sunrise. You know they will."

"That's for a military jury to decide."

Jack turned his eyes toward Georg. "Come to think of it, Captain, you needn't concern yourself with a trial for this young fella. I've heard about the justice handed out to young men like Georg here in those camps. How long do you think he'll last amongst his own back at Camp Trinidad once word gets out—and it will get out—that he betrayed one of his officers to save my life?"

"We can provide protection. You have my word on that. Mr. Carson, I just came from a memorial service for two of my men at Camp Trinidad. Your young friend here and his cohorts left them dead in a ditch overlooking your ranch two days ago. If you think I have any sympathy for this young man, you are sadly mistaken."

Instantly, Jack came back. "Colonel Von Toth and the dead POWs are responsible for all the killing, Captain. Georg here is a witness to the deaths of those guards and the Koivunens. And I watched while the colonel did in old Trapper Anderson."

"You're saying he can prove his innocence in the slaying of my men?" asked MacLean.

Jack lifted his chin and looked at MacLean. "He gave me his word, and that's good enough for me."

There was movement on the bed and both men turned to look at Georg.

"Mr. Carson," said Georg, his voice steady, his handsome face sad, "please don't involve yourself any further on my account. You'd only be putting yourself at risk. I'll go back with the captain."

Jack ignored him, and turned to stare at MacLean with penetrating eyes. "Tell me, Captain, you're a fighting man with a sworn duty to obey orders. Put yourself in Georg's shoes. What would *you* have done if your superior had forced *you* along on an escape attempt you wanted nothing to do with?"

MacLean took a deep breath, held it, and bit his upper lip. Putting his hands again behind his back, he shifted his feet and looked away. "That doesn't wash, Carson."

"Answer me," Jack said. "What would you have done?"

MacLean paused and looked at the floor, then past Jack and out the window. "I guess I would have done what any good soldier would. Obey the order and then face the consequences just as though it were my own decision. Just like young Georg here." He looked directly at Jack. "Listen, I don't make the rules. I'm just here to do my job."

"Well then, get out and give me and my family the five minutes you offered us!"

MacLean glanced at Georg, then at Jack, and turned to leave. He opened the door and saw the worried looks on the faces of the Carson children who were waiting in the hall, drew a deep breath, closed the door, and turned back to face Jack. He stared at him for a long moment.

"I'll need a statement from you that you saw Georg Dreschler die out in the wilderness."

Jack couldn't hold back a broad smile. "Yes, sir," he said. "You'll have it!"

"One more thing. This little ruse won't stand the test of time—not without forged papers, professionally done, that say Dave Mankowski is an American citizen." He hesitated, looked down at the cap in his hands, turning the cap as if examining it for stains. "There's a POW at Trinidad who's a skilled forger. I'll set him to work on it this evening. Come see me in the morning."

Jack came across the room and reached to shake the captain's hand. "Thank you, sir." He tightened his grip and gave one more hard shake. "Thank you!"

MacLean looked past Jack's shoulder at a bewildered Georg. "Welcome to America, Mr. Mankowski."

"Thank you, sir." Georg raised himself to shake MacLean's hand.

The captain looked at Jack again. "Should anything go wrong with this little masquerade of yours," he said, "this conversation never occurred."

Jack grinned. "I've never before set eyes on you."

Jack followed MacLean out the door and, still smiling broadly, waved his children back in.

EPILOGUE

Georg Dreschler did indeed finish out the war as Dave Mankowski, Jack's hired hand. But he never did go his own way afterward, save for a short postwar trip to Germany to convince his war-ravaged parents to immigrate to Colorado. His love for the Carson family in general and for Cassie in particular led to his planting deep roots in the rich Segundo soil. He lives there to this day in blessed wedlock with Cassie and in amicable partnership with Josh and Wade, tending to the daily affairs of the famous Carson Ranch.

1496064

Made in the USA